BUILT TO LAST

HOT DAM HOMES
BOOK THREE

HARPER ROBSON

Updated 4.22.2025

CONTENTS

One of the Main Characters in *Built To Last* was seriously injured while serving in the US Military, and it briefly describes the event. The book also references one character's traumatic childhood with an addicted and neglectful parent. Lastly, there is a character in the book who is suffering from Alzheimer's disease.

Please be cautious if these subjects are difficult for you.

I've done my best to represent all of the above as sensitively and accurately as possible, so please forgive any errors.

Thanks so much for reading and I hope you enjoy Sam & Tyler's story!

CHAPTER 1

TYLER

"Fucking hell," I mutter, clenching the steering wheel tightly as I sit in a miles-long line of traffic on Interstate 5. The commute between Seattle and Tacoma can feel long even on a sunny day, but in the winter, thanks to Washington's dark skies and drenching rain, it becomes completely unreasonable. I'll be getting home way later than I planned, which sucks donkey balls. Because I have to be careful with my sleep schedule, I'll have almost no time to wind down before I'll need to take my sleep meds and go to bed.

Before I can decide whether to give up and take the next exit so I can wait out the traffic somewhere, the dashboard screen lights up with a text from my boss. I've worked at Hot Dam Homes, a small, family-owned renovation company, since shortly after getting home from my tour with the Army in Afghanistan. Mason Campbell, who owns the company with his brother, Dylan, is a great guy who genuinely thinks of the company as an extension of his family. It sounds stupid and cliché, but he really does believe it, and it shows in how he treats us. Needless to say, I consider myself lucky as fuck to have ended up working for them.

> Mason: Team meeting tomorrow afternoon. Dinner at pub after. Sorry for late notice. Can u make it?

Spending the afternoon stuck in a meeting room instead of being able to move around and use my hands isn't high on my list of favorite things, but Mason and Dylan are amazing bosses, and they must have something important to talk to us about if they're calling a meeting on such late notice.

"I can be there," I say slowly and clearly so the voice-to-text software picks up my words.

> Mason: Great. Stay at our place if u want to drink. Bring your stuff.

"Okay," I respond, smiling to myself. Mason is like a mother hen. I'm the only one of the group who lives so friggin' far away, and he's always concerned about me getting home from work safely, especially in the winter when the weather can be bad.

As predicted, I get home later than I'd like. I hate living all the way in Tacoma, but housing closer to Seattle is insane. I could get a roommate, but that thought gives me the hee-bie-jeebies for a whole host of reasons. Besides, Tacoma might not be glamorous, but at least it's familiar. I grew up here, and I've had so many changes to my life over the past few years it's not a bad thing to have surroundings I know like the back of my hand, even if they're not luxurious.

After getting into my crappy little apartment and locking the door behind me, the first thing I do is take out my hearing aids, letting out a big sigh of relief. The sensation is kind of like taking off a pair of uncomfortable shoes after being on your feet all day. As helpful and necessary as my hearing aids are, I'm not sure I'll ever get used to having something stuck in my ears all day, every day.

Wandering into my small kitchen, I decide to stick a frozen dinner in the microwave since I'm too tired for anything else.

I really need to make some kind of plan for moving closer to Seattle. The drive back and forth feels like it gets more exhausting every day. At some point, I won't have a choice because I can't sacrifice my mental health over a stressful daily commute. Prior to losing my hearing, I don't think it would have been as big a problem, but driving requires a lot more concentration now, so it's more tiring.

After scarfing back my mediocre dinner while watching an old episode of *Brooklyn Nine-Nine*, I force myself to shut off the TV and climb into bed. I've learned to be strict with my sleep routine. The trauma from being blown up by a roadside IED and losing almost all my hearing resulted in severe nightmares for a long time. But after I started seeing my psychiatrist, Derek, and followed his suggestions by taking the meds he recommended, the nightmares tapered off. Nowadays, they normally only happen if I slack off with my routine or if my stress level gets too high.

After brushing my teeth, I shut out the light and grab my e-reader. I started reading gay romance novels while I was deployed. Before I had my e-reader, I didn't even know there was an entire genre of books devoted to queer romance. I don't really think of myself as the romantic type, but those books got me through a lot of very long nights. I always had to be careful not to let my bunkmates see the sometimes cheesy beefcake images adorning the covers of my favorite books. It was bad enough they all gave me a hard time for being bisexual; I didn't want to add more fuel to the fire. I know a lot of the guys were truly kidding around with me and didn't really have hostile intentions, but there were at least a couple who set off a few red flags. You can never be too careful as a non-straight member of the military, so I liked being able to keep my preferences, for books and everything else, to myself. Between reading and drawing with the few little art supplies I managed to bring with me, I was able to keep sane.

After only a few pages of my latest read, an extra-steamy story about a dragon shifter bodyguard who falls in love with the human he's protecting, I'm fighting to keep my eyes open, so I close the cover on my reader and let sleep pull me under.

CHAPTER 2

SAM

Pulling into the Hot Dam Homes parking lot, I'm feeling good, having just finished a major renovation job that wasn't exactly a walk in the park. The only thing left is for Mason or Dylan to conduct the final inspection and get the client's sign-off. The nitpicky old couple were a challenge to work with, constantly changing their minds and finding fault with everything, then demanding discounts for every imaginary deficiency. I think they're finally happy now though, and I'm proud of how I handled them.

I've worked for my cousin, Dylan Campbell, since he started his small home-renovation company a few years ago. I'm a landscape designer by training, but I like the overall work of construction and general contracting, so I've stuck around a long time. Dylan's brother, Mason, who also happens to be my best friend, has also worked for HDH since the beginning. A couple of years ago, he bought into the company and became co-owner. It wasn't a surprise, since Dylan had always wanted the company to be a partnership between himself and Mason; it just took Mason a while to commit. But after he met the love of his life and got settled into a perfect domestic world, he was finally ready to take the plunge to become a full partner with his brother.

What shocked the hell out of me was how crazy jealous I was of their new partnership. I *never* thought I wanted the kind of responsibility being co-owner would bring, but seeing Mason doing it, actually growing up and doing the full-on adulting thing, triggered something in me. I found myself craving the extra responsibility, but the company is too small to have three of us as equal partners, so I remain their faithful employee. It's fine, really. My friendship with Mason is one of the most important things in my life, and even though there have been times when him being my boss has felt weird to both of us, we've both worked hard to keep our relationship normal. Lately, though, I feel like there's been a distance between us that hasn't been there before.

Shutting off the truck and hopping out, I give my head a shake, as if the annoying thoughts trying to upend my good mood will tumble out and fall to the ground. I'm not sure what this unexpected meeting is about, but it must be something good because they want to take the whole crew out for dinner and drinks after. It's been a long week, so I'm more than happy to show up. Thank god it's Friday night, as I can definitely use a little wind-down, and I won't have to worry about having to drag myself out of bed at the ass-crack of dawn to work.

A bunch of the younger employees have already arrived and are milling around the back of the meeting room. Kylie, the office manager, has set out sodas and water and a package of those stupid-addictive chocolate chip cookies from Costco, so everyone will get their late-afternoon sugar rush.

"Hey, assholes." I grin, slapping Kevin, one of our newest hires, on the shoulder. "What's happening?"

We chat for a few minutes before Mason and Dylan come in, Dylan followed closely by

Alexis, one of his rescued Labrador retrievers, who shadows him pretty much wherever he goes. She heads to her dog bed in the corner and turns in a circle three times before settling down with a contented sigh as Dylan and Mason take their seats.

"Hey, all," Mason starts with a friendly smile. Dylan doesn't talk much at these meetings. He's autistic, and peopling isn't his thing. He's really into the design and build aspects of the business like the engineering and architecture, while Mason handles the more people-oriented stuff like sales and customer relations. It works, since HDH has been really successful.

"I know we all want to get over to Harley's for a couple of drinks and some greasy pub food, so I'll get right to the point." Mason stops to clear his throat before continuing. "As some of you already know, a few months back, we put in a bid for a huge job to rebuild an old vacation resort on the coast, close to Ocean Shores. The new owners want to turn it into a super-exclusive, luxury getaway destination. We weren't sure if they'd even look at us, since we've never tackled anything that big before, but we found out today that we won the job!"

The excitement in Mason's voice is contagious, and even Dylan is grinning widely. A wave of excitement moves through the room, and there are even a few cheers and some scattered whoops.

"If things go as well as we hope, this could be our entry into doing more of those kinds of vacation homes. Eventually, we'd like to expand HDH so we can cover the coast, as well as east into the Cascades." He continues. "We want to be the go-to for high-end clients when they want to update their cabins in the mountains and their vacation homes at the beach. This job will be a good taste to see if that's something we really want to pursue." Some of the others exchange looks, possibly wondering why Mason called an "all hands on deck" meeting just to announce we'd won a new job.

"So, all this means a couple of things. The best news is that you're all going to see a bump in your profit sharing once we get rolling on this project, so you should be excited about that." He smiles widely, and there are some happy murmurs. I swear, HDH is a fucking unicorn. What other small construction company gives every employee profit sharing? As well as a healthy benefits package and a retirement savings plan? It's a place I'm proud to be associated with. I really can't imagine my life if I wasn't working here, being with these people every day. But I'm going to have to do a lot of thinking about exactly that, and very soon.

I haven't told a soul, but I got a call last week from an old friend I went to school with, Shane Elliston. He moved down to Southern California a couple of years ago and started a landscape and pool design business. He's been so successful that he needs help managing it, and he called to see if I'd be interested in coming to work with him. His plan was to try things out for six months, and if it went well, I'd have the option to buy in, meaning Shane and I would be equal partners. It's a fucking amazing opportunity, and I was floored when he spelled it out for me, but I told him I needed time to think about it. He understood and asked for an answer in the next couple of months. I know I've got loads of time to make the decision, but I haven't been able to focus on anything else since our conversation.

I've lived in Western Washington my entire life, and my roots run deep here. Even though I'm an only child, I'm incredibly close to my huge extended family. Moving away would be a huge shock to my system, and until the last year or so, I'd never even considered it. But with the way things have been feeling different between Mason and me lately, I'm not sure if there's room for me at Hot Dam Homes anymore. And that's only my work life. If you were to take into account the pathetic state of my love life, or lack thereof, you might wonder why the hell I feel anchored to Seattle at all.

"The owner has visions of the resort becoming a hidden jewel along the Pacific Northwest coast," Mason's saying. "He's a big-deal Hollywood producer, and he wants to run the resort when he retires. I guess it's always been his wife's dream to do this, and he's sparing no expense to get top-quality everything. The reason he hired us is because of our local knowledge. He's serious about not wanting to be some giant douche-canoe gajillionaire who comes into a small town and changes everything. He wants this place to be super exclusive, a place where A-listers can come and be left alone. The location is perfect for that kind of thing since it's sort of hidden away, off the highway a bit. It's on this little peninsula, with the buildings sitting right on the cliff's edge. The views are just insane." Mason is as excited as a puppy with a bone. It's ridiculously cute.

"Anyway, I can tell you're wondering why in hell we called you in here for this, right?" He grins, and there are a few chuckles around the room. He might be the boss, but he's still one of the guys. I don't think Mason knows how to be any other way, and his employees love him for it.

"This job is critical to HDH, so we need to get it right since it will be like a living business card for some very high-net-worth clients. Normally, for a job like this, we would handle planning and coordinating, and then we'd subcontract out most of the work to local guys. But I want to try something different." He pauses for effect here, and I chuckle inwardly. My cousin has picked up a few storytelling tips from his actor and soon-to-be screenwriter husband, Jackson Cullen. He's giving this story the full dramatic treatment, and everyone in the room, myself included, is hanging off every word.

"We decided to call this a *Hot Dam Homes Signature Project*. That means anyone putting a finger on this job is either a full-time HDH employee or is someone we've already worked with and can vouch for. We know the quality of the work you all do, and that's what makes our reputation so stellar. What all this means is that we have some really cool opportunities coming up for anyone who's interested in working out on the coast for a few weeks at a time on this job. It's bigger than anything we've done before, so it's going to be new and different. There's going to be a ton of stuff for all of us to learn, and it would be good for everyone to spend some time there." Mason pauses, and the room explodes with excited chatter for a minute before he holds a hand up, laughing. "I know there will be a shitload of questions, so let's go one at a time so everyone can hear the answers."

The room quiets down, and Brad, one of the senior guys, speaks first.

"Are you going to be staying out there for the whole job?" he asks.

"Good question, and no, I won't be out there for the whole time. Pretty sure Jackson would have my head in a vise for that." He grins sheepishly. "But our plan is to have one or two guys move out there for the whole time to act as forepersons, overseeing all the moving parts." Brad nods, satisfied with the answer.

After a few more questions, the meeting starts to naturally break up, and Mason and Dylan start to get up from their chairs. "Just one more thing," Mason says, gathering some papers from the table. "If any of you are interested in living out at the coast for a while and taking on the foreperson job I talked about, come talk to me, and we'll see what we can do. I trust each one of you to do a great job, and this is a fantastic opportunity for anyone who might be looking to spend some time out of Seattle."

My mind wanders as Mason answers more questions that pop up as people start getting their stuff ready to go. I don't want to admit it, but I'm a little hurt he and Dylan didn't let me in on this news before telling the rest of the company. I know I'm not officially a partner, but I've always been kind of treated as a "number two." I snort inwardly at that and then roll my eyes at myself. God, I'm such a child. But if my status as Hot Dam Homes' "number two" is fading, maybe it's another sign I need to be changing my life up. California would at least be warm and sunny.

I wonder who they're going to want to live out there as their point people. Like he mentioned, Mason isn't going to want to be away from home for that long, especially since the worst-kept secret around is that he and Jackson have been searching for a surrogate as they try to start a family, so he won't be doing any long-term traveling. Dylan's partner, Reed, is an ER doctor here in town, plus they have a little hobby farm out in the eastern suburbs. They can't leave for extended periods without having someone come in to care for their animals. What that probably means is that they're going to want me to move out there. Which, honestly, sounds amazing. A few months away from Seattle and out of the comfortable family nest might be just what I need to work myself out of the funk I've been in for the last few months. Maybe I'll be able to get some clarity on what, and where, I want my future to be. Obviously, Ocean Shores isn't as far away as SoCal, but it's still further away than anywhere else I've lived. Considering I'm pushing forty, maybe it's time I expand my horizons and do a little adulting of my own.

Over the last few years, I've watched both Mason and Dylan find their person. Neither of them really thought they'd be the type to settle down. Mason spent years in a toxic and traumatic relationship, and it took him a long time to recover. Dylan, being autistic, never believed he'd be able to connect with someone on that level. But they've each managed to find a partner who is perfect for them. Don't get me wrong, I'm incredibly happy for both of them. But when we were kids, I was the one who harbored secret dreams of getting married and having a big family one day. I've never had grand career ambitions. I know that's not a typical little boy's dream, but the heart wants what it wants, I guess. I've always wanted the whole deal, right down to the white picket fence.

Even as a teen, when I realized I liked both girls and guys, that vision I had for my future didn't change much. My family is incredibly supportive, so I knew I would want a big family whether my partner was a woman or a man. But I haven't found my person, and believe me, I've tried real hard. Serial dater, thy name is Sam. Maybe the universe really is sending me a message. Maybe it's time I start imagining a different future.

Shaking my head, I try to clear out my confusing thoughts as Mason finishes answering questions and announces we're heading out to our local hangout, Harley's.

CHAPTER 3

TYLER

As Mason wraps up the meeting, Kev, one of the guys I've been working with lately, puts a hand on my shoulder.

I turn to face him, and he waits until I can see his mouth before speaking. "Dude, you coming to Harley's?" he asks and then continues before I can answer. "Parking is always a bitch down there on the waterfront. Why don't I give you a lift?"

"Sure, that sounds great," I say, giving him an easy smile. Kev can be a little immature sometimes, but he's a good guy. Like everyone at Hot Dam Homes, he's great about making sure I'm looking at him before he speaks to me so I can lip-read. Just one of a million small and large reasons I love working with this company.

As we follow everyone out of the conference room, I sneak a glance over at Sam Campbell. His expression is bright as sunshine as he chats with some of the others. Because he hasn't noticed me, I treat myself to a nice, long look, taking in his wavy brown hair and brown eyes surrounded by the cutest laugh lines. I've always thought Sam was hot as hell, but he looks particularly gorgeous today. He has to keep running a hand through his hair to keep it out of his eyes, which is strangely sexy. He must have changed after he finished up at his jobsite, as his normally grubby, paint-stained jeans and random concert tee have been replaced with clean jeans that fit him like a second skin. The way they spread over his ass and wrap his strong thighs perfectly make my mouth water. His heather-gray Henley is just tight enough to highlight the shape of his arms, and I immediately start picturing what his abs must look like underneath that fabric. The man is a total smokeshow.

I don't know him well, but that's my fault, not his. When I first started at HDH, I hadn't been home from deployment long, and I was struggling to adapt to my hearing loss. I didn't talk much to anyone, although if I'm honest, that's not a huge change. I was never a big talker, even before I lost my hearing. Sam tried to draw me out a lot during those first months, but after I repeatedly shut him down, he backed off. Which just shows what a great guy he is; he didn't push me when he realized I was uncomfortable. The only problem is that now, I'd *love* to get to know him better, but I'm way too socially awkward to do anything about it, and seriously, there's no way a guy like Sam would ever want to be with someone like me.

I wouldn't say I'm completely at ease with the whole deafness thing now, but I'm a lot more relaxed about it than I was back then. Hearing aids have made a big difference, and while I'll never be able to hear the world the way I used to, technology keeps giving us more and more ways to adapt to being deaf. There is also an entire community of deaf and hard of hearing people out there who I can reach out to for help. Since I still have some of my hearing, I haven't been forced to learn a sign language like ASL, although I'd like to if I could ever find the time. I'd like to make more connections within the D/deaf community. It would be nice to have people to talk to who just get it without me having to explain anything.

Just as Kevin and I are getting to the door, Sam must sense someone looking at him because he looks up, and our eyes lock, like something out of one of my romance novels. I bite my lip to stop from snorting a laugh, because what the hell kind of ridiculous thought is that, and give him an awkward half-wave thing before following Kevin out the door.

It's a typical January night in Seattle, rain absolutely pelting down. The wind is blowing like a son of a bitch, driving the rain into our faces so it feels like we're getting stabbed with thousands of tiny needles as we jog across the parking lot and into the pub. We're first to arrive, so we get ourselves situated by pulling a few tables together, and Kev goes to let the staff know there will be a bunch of us coming in while he grabs the first round.

When he returns to the table, he hands me a ginger ale. I guess I've managed to get to know these guys enough so that they know what I drink, or don't, when we go out.

I'm not a complete tectotaler, but I don't touch booze if I'm driving. It's a rule I gave myself when alcohol began to feel like something

I couldn't live without. When I first got back from deployment, I got into the dangerous habit of drinking myself to sleep every night. It was pretty much the only coping mechanism I had, since growing up, that was the only way I ever saw adults deal with hard shit. My mom always believed the answer to any problem could be found at the bottom of a bottle of cheap vodka. And even though she never found it, she kept looking for years, which is a big part of the reason she landed in a care home with severe dementia when she's only in her mid-fifties.

The rest of the HDH gang spills into the bar, and it's a lively crowd. To make things even more interesting, the rest of the Campbell clan shows up shortly after everyone else, which is fun, although it can be a little overwhelming. In addition to Mason and Dylan, there's Jackson, Mason's husband, who used to be an action movie star; Reed, Dylan's partner, who is also a smoking-hot ER doctor; Mason and Dylan's sister, Grace; and her husband, Derek, who, ironically, is my therapist and is basically responsible for me getting the job at Hot Dam Homes.

The Campbells are so different from my own family it's mind-boggling. They're a big, boisterous, fun group who clearly enjoys spending time together. My family, on the other hand, consisted of my mom, who, if she was around, was usually drunk or stoned, and my older brother, Aaron, and calling us "dysfunctional" would be a huge compliment. I'm not sure there's a word to describe how fucked-up we were. But I like seeing how the Campbells interact with each other. It feels like watching a movie since it feels so far out of my reach. They're always teasing each other and laughing, telling jokes and stories. It makes me happy and sad at the same time. Sad because I never got to experience that kind of family, but happy to see they exist in the real world. It's nice to have proof that happy families don't only exist in Hollywood fairy tales.

A couple of hours later, I'm considering heading out, but before I can excuse myself, Mason comes and sits in the chair beside me.

"Hey, Ty, how are things going, man? How's the Patel job coming along?" he asks, referring to the job I've been working on this week, a big renovation in one of the older, wealthy suburbs. The clients are really nice, but they have incredibly high standards, which can be intimidating.

"I'm good, Mason, thanks," I say. "And things at the Patel place are great. I think they're really happy with what we've got done so far, plus we're on schedule to finish early, so they're excited about that."

"Awesome. I heard things were going well there—that's great, Tyler. Impressing Mr. and Mrs. Patel isn't easy." He shoots me a pleased grin, and I get a nice little rush of pride. I love being good at my job.

"So, Tyler, I'd really like you to consider taking the long-term position out at Ocean Shores. It would be great experience for you, and you'll knock it out of the park."

I blink at him, my jaw dropping open before I realize it, and I snap it shut. "What?" I ask. There's no way I heard him right, which can happen when I'm in a place with a lot of background noise. I glance down at my phone, which has an app that acts like closed-captioning for live conversations and is super useful in situations like this. It does occasionally screw things up though, similar to autocorrect, and it's led to some rather unfortunate misunderstandings in the past. My app shows that Mason said what I thought he did, but it can't be right.

"I'm sorry, I think I got that wrong. What did you say?" I ask.

Mason looks like he's choking back a laugh. "I think you got the message right, Ty. I said I want you to think about taking that foreperson job on the coast. I think you're ready for it."

I'm so shocked I can't reply for a minute, and Mason stops trying to hold back and lets out a chuckle. He stands and places a hand on my shoulder. "I won't force you it if you're really not comfortable. But I know you're ready to take this on. Dylan does too. Think about it over the weekend, okay?"

"Oh! I... Uhmmm... Yeah, I will..." I stammer, totally dumbfounded.

Mason drains the last of his beer. "I gotta get going," he says. "But promise me you'll think on it. Oh, and you should stay in our guesthouse tonight—don't drive all the way home in this shit weather!"

He gives my shoulder a squeeze and turns to go, leaving me stunned as he heads for the door, where Jackson's waiting for him, a ball cap pulled down low to cover his striking blond hair and blue eyes.

Sucking in a breath, I turn back to the table and find the open chair across from me has been filled by none other than the gorgeous Sam Campbell. As if my mind wasn't completely scrambled from that conversation with Mason, now I've got one of the hottest guys I know sitting two feet away from me. I swallow hard and push the conversation with Mason out of my mind, putting a pin in it until I can take it out later to examine it. It's a skill I perfected while I was in Afghanistan, when there was often shit on my mind, but if I allowed myself to lose focus on what was happening in front of me, I'd be dead.

We spend a while longer sitting around chatting, and I have a good time in spite of myself. My instinct is usually to turn down these invites for after-work drinks, but when I say yes, I'm always glad I came. When people start trickling out to head home, I glance at my watch. Sam, who's still sitting across from me, notices.

"Late for a hot date?" He grins.

I snicker. "Unfortunately, no. I've got a long drive home, so I should probably head out."

Sam gives me a puzzled look. "You're still living in Tacoma? I thought you moved up closer a while ago?"

I shake my head. "No, I was going to move in with one of the new guys, but he found a cheaper place with some college kids. It was a better fit for him."

I hadn't been all that upset when the potential roommate situation had fallen through a few months ago. While I wouldn't miss the shitty commute every day, the thought of sharing a small apartment with someone I don't know very well makes me break out in hives. The few years of living like sardines in a can while I was in the Army only made my natural desire for privacy more intense. I also worry about people being annoyed by some of the adaptive shit I need to use, like the lights flashing for the doorbell and always having to have closed-captions on the TV. None of the guys I work with have ever given any indication they would be like that, but you never know. So, the whole roommate scene is something I'd like to avoid if I can.

"Oh, wow," Sam says thoughtfully. "How come you're not staying at Mason and Jax's guest pad, then? It's still crap weather out there, and their guesthouse is plush, as you know since you helped build it!" His eyes twinkle as he looks at me over the rim of his pint glass.

I laugh. "Yeah, Mason offered me their guest-house, but I'd rather get home to my own bed.

Just a creature of habit, I guess." I shrug, feeling a little self-conscious.

"Oh, okay. Well, I know for certain Mason and Jax would love for you to stay there, but no worries if you gotta head home." Sam drains the last of his beer. "I'm actually going to head out too. Where'd you park?"

"I left my car at the office. Got a ride with Kev, but I haven't seen him for a while," I say, glancing around for my ride.

Sam chuckles. "Mmm, well, I'm not sure he's going to be willing to leave just yet." He shoots a look across the bar, and I follow his gaze to the pool tables, where it appears Kevin has his hands full of pretty girl. She's leaning over the pool table to take a shot, and he's apparently giving her "lessons." He's bent over so he's almost on top of her, his crotch pressed into her ass, which is barely covered by a tiny white skirt, as he helps her line up her shot.

I snort a laugh and shake my head. "Right, then. I guess I'm calling an Uber."

Sam waves his hand at me dismissively. "Nah, I'll give you a ride to the office. I gotta go past there on my way home."

"Oh. Okay, sure," I say. Truthfully, the thought of spending a little more time in Sam's sunny presence sounds good, plus I know he'll never let me call an Uber. This crowd takes care of each other, and the older guys are all pretty protective of the younger crowd.

For some people, having your employer be so concerned with making sure you get home from work safely every night might feel intrusive, but I don't mind. It's been a really long time since anyone was particularly concerned about my well-being. Honestly, I'm not sure anyone has ever cared all that much. My mom was always either wasted or not around. Plus, whichever man she happened to be latched onto at the time always took priority over her kids. Keeping her man happy was always job one. My older brother, Aaron, cared about me, but he was just a kid, only seven years older than me. It wasn't the same as having a parent.

Being mothered by Mason and the rest of the guys at work is a nice novelty. It makes me feel good to know someone would notice if I didn't show up for work. The guys in the military cared, but that was part of the job. No one at Hot Dam Homes has any obligation to give a shit about what I do once I'm off the clock, but they do. It feels more family-like than anything I've had before.

"Um, sure. That'd be great," I say, hoping I sound confident.

Sam gives me a crooked smile that causes my dick to twitch in my jeans. "Okay, just give me a minute to grab my stuff, and we'll head out."

CHAPTER 4

SAM

Opening the door of Harley's to get outside is like getting slapped with a wet towel. The rain is coming down hard, and in classic PNW style, it's not exactly 'falling' as much as flying sideways through the air, so it hits you square in the face if you happen to be walking into the wind.

"Ugh," Tyler and I both grunt, each of us grabbing for the hoods on our jackets—one winter accessory you don't want to be without here in Seattle. We tend to scorn anyone who carries an umbrella in these parts, but a proper hood that can keep the rain out of your face is standard operating equipment.

We scurry across the parking lot to where my pickup is parked, jumping inside and slamming the doors shut behind us. Once we're inside, we exchange a glance, both laughing. It's such a classic Seattle moment—cold, wet, dark, and, to me anyway, it feels like home. This kind of weather is part of my genetic makeup. It's one of those things everyone who's not from around here hates, but I kind of love the wildness of the weather here.

"Whoever ends up doing that new project on the coast better get used to this stuff," I laugh. "I haven't spent the winter out there, but I've heard the big storms at this time of year can get crazy." I start the truck and blast the heat onto the windshield to clear the fogged-up windows,

"Yeah, I guess you're right," Tyler says noncommittally. He's chewing on his bottom lip like it's done something to offend him, and I have the strangest urge to reach over and pull it out from between his teeth.

"Everything okay?" I ask, and he turns to me with a sunny smile that seems to be hiding something, but I can't tell what.

"Yup, all good. Just ready for bed, is all."

I bite my tongue to stop myself from suggesting yet again that he stay at Mason's guesthouse. He's clearly tired, and I genuinely don't think he should drive all the way back home in this crap weather so late at night, but he's a grown-ass man. Nothing I can do to stop him if that's what he wants to do.

"Hey, Tyler, I hope you know Mason's serious about wanting you to use their place. He's not just saying it," I say. "I mean, obviously, we know you're capable of getting yourself home, but it is a long drive after a long week in shitty weather. It doesn't mean we think you can't take care of yourself or anything."

"I know, I appreciate it. Really, I do," he says, giving me a shy smile. "But I'm totally fine, I promise."

I take in his blue eyes and notice the light smattering of freckles spread across his nose. I try to ignore how my heart skips a beat and warmth floods my body. But I look away quickly as memories of him shutting me down many times flood my brain.

"I won't pressure you anymore, but just so you know, Mason isn't treating you any differently than he would anyone else. He's just kind of a nurturing guy. And he'd be genuinely thrilled if someone would ever take him up on his offer to stay at their guesthouse. I swear, the man's always trying to get someone to stay there." I grin at him.

I've been intrigued with Tyler Ritchie since he started with HDH a couple of years ago. His first job with us was the job where Mason met his now husband, Jackson. Mason told me one of the first times he realized he was falling for Jackson was when he found him sitting with Tyler one afternoon as Tyler was tearing out one of the bathrooms. Jax had just sauntered in and was shooting the shit with the young veteran who was newly hearing-impaired and was obviously still adjusting both to being out of the military and to life with his hearing challenge. Tyler relaxed immediately around Jax and even started joking around with him. Jax does have a way of making people relax and trust him. I still think it's sweet that Mason thinks of that moment as the one where he really fell for Jax.

As we sit, waiting for the windows to defog, my phone pings with a traffic alert, so I grab it to check the details.

"Um, Tyler, I hate to be the bearer of bad news, but I think you're gonna be staying at the guesthouse tonight after all," I say, reading from the screen.

"What?" he asks, looking surprised.

"Looks like I-5 is closed south of the airport because of a big pileup."

"Ah, shit," Tyler mutters, grabbing his own phone. "Ugh, you're right. They're telling people to stay off the roads if they can. I guess there are a lot of trees down on the side roads, so everything's a mess. Crap," he mutters.

"Did you want me to drop you at your car or take you straight over to Mason's place?" I ask. He's probably pissed that he won't be able to get home tonight, but I'm not above feeling relieved that he won't need to drive all that way in this storm.

He sighs, letting his head fall back into the seat behind him. "Whatever's easier for you," he says, looking slightly defeated. Rather than arguing, I decide I'll take him to Mason's place and make sure he can get into the guesthouse and get settled in. There's something about Tyler that makes me want to protect him, which is weird since I've never had those instincts before.

It's only about a ten-minute drive to Mason and Jackson's gorgeous home on Lake Washington. I park the pickup outside the separate building housing a garage and workshop with a guest flat over it, which they built last year. Instead of slowing down, the storm seems to have picked up in intensity since we walked out of the pub, and the wind is fucking fierce. Mason and Jackson's place is nestled into a group of tall fir trees, and they're groaning loudly as they get pummeled and pushed around by the wind. This storm seems unusually strong, and the loud creaking and occasional cracking noises coming from the forest are making me a little nervous.

CHAPTER 5

TYLER

For a second, I thought Sam was messing with me when he told me the highway was closed, but I realized pretty damn quickly that it was no joke.

I helped Mason and Jax build their separate workshop/garage/guest apartment last summer, so I know it's a great place to crash for the night. Their entire home is incredible. If I was a rich movie star like Jackson Cullen, I'd totally buy a house exactly like this. It's not enormous, more like the size of a big suburban family home, as opposed to one of the giant mansions that line Lake Washington. I mean, Bill Gates lives not far from here, so they have some pretty interesting neighbors.

They have a pool and a hot tub and a small sports court, as well as plenty of room for their dogs to play in the yard, but it doesn't feel pretentious. It's set back from the road, nestled in a grove of towering Douglas fir trees, and somehow this house feels like it belongs here. Like it was meant to be in this space all along.

I open the door of the pickup, and the wind catches it, ripping it out of my hand and blowing it wide open. The sound of the rain and the trees rubbing and brushing together in the heavy wind is loud enough that even I can hear them.

"Jesus," I yell over at Sam, who's sitting on the other side of the console, looking at me wide-eyed after the damn truck door nearly got ripped off.

Sam shouts something at me that I can't catch with all the wind and other background noise, but when he starts getting out of the truck as well, I figure he must have said he'll come up with me.

I step out of the cab and turn to shut the door, impressed with the strength of these winds because I have to use a ton of force to close it.

The entry to the guest suite is up a set of stairs at the side of the garage. Thankfully, there are battery-powered safety lights lining the steps. We run up, shielding our faces from the driving rain. Once we're at the top, Sam reaches around me and punches in a code to unlock the door, and we step inside the cozy suite.

As soon as he shuts the door behind us, it feels like we've been transported into another dimension. Mason and Jax must have turned on the heat because it's toasty warm in here. It feels amazing since we're both soaked to the skin.

"Jesus H. Christ on a piece of toast," Sam says loudly, and I chuckle. He sometimes busts out these silly dad-like jokes and expressions, and they're super adorable. Not that I would know what a dad is like, but I imagine Sam is the epitome of what a great dad would be. He's so solid and reliable. You know if you need him for anything, he'll be there. The man would literally give you the shirt off his back, and he'd do his best to make you comfortable while he did it. All the members of the Campbell family are amazing, and they all have that sort of calm, steady presence, but something about Sam is different... He's just, I don't know, more dependable or something.

I wrench myself back from my thoughts as he slips off his Gore-Tex jacket and shakes some of the water off.

"God, I feel like I've been standing in a cold shower," he mutters loud enough that I can hear him. "Want me to text Mason and Jax to let them know you'll be staying?" he says as we both toe off our wet work boots.

"Yeah, sure," I say. Walking into the small kitchen area, I flip on the lights. In a testament to the modern electrical grid, the power is still on, even though the wind is blowing like I've never seen in my life.

I look around, admiring the small but comfortable space.

"Not bad for a little guest pad, right?" Sam asks, following me into the kitchen as I nosily start checking stuff out. "I'm pretty sure they built it so they can have a live-in nanny," he says, looking down at his phone as he types.

"Oh, really?" I ask, surprised. I hadn't really thought about the fact that Mason and Jax might have a family. Although, why wouldn't they, I guess? They're both great guys and will make amazing dads someday.

"Yeah. They've both always wanted kids. Mason never used to talk about it though. Before

Jax, he was more of a 'play the field and sow my wild oats' kind of guy. But he told me last year he's always wanted kids." Sam gets a funny look in his eye for a second. It looks like it's... wistful, maybe? But a second later, the look disappears, replaced by his usual sunny expression. He sets his phone on the counter and smiles. "They've already started working with an agency to match them with a surrogate, so I guess that could happen anytime." He shakes his head again, and a little smile appears on his face before he turns around to open the fridge. He bends over to grab something, and fucking hell, I want to hurdle right over this countertop and take a bite of his gorgeous ass. He looks at me over his shoulder, his eyes twinkling as he realizes I'm checking him out. *Damn.* Caught red-handed ogling the boss. *Nice work, Tyler.*

"I know you're not a big drinker, but since you're in for the night, want one?" he asks but then looks embarrassed, standing up straight. "I mean, unless you want to get to bed? Sorry, that was kind of presumptuous... I can totally head out if you'd rather go to sleep." His cheeks are flushed, and it makes me want to hug him.

"No, of course, stay for a while!" I say, and I feel a few little butterflies take flight in my belly.

Maybe a drink will help me relax, and I'll lose some of this social anxiety that's got me feeling jumpy as a jackrabbit.

I have zero idea how a guy like Sam is still single. I know he's either bi or pansexual since he used to have a girlfriend, but I know he occasionally dates guys. I haven't seen him with anyone for a while though. By anyone's standards, the guy is a fucking catch. He's hot AF, and as I mentioned before, he's the most steady, reliable person I've ever met. He's like a soft, cozy blanket of a person.

He turns back to the fridge and grabs two beers. He passes one to me, and we both twist off the caps as we head over to the big, cushy sectional. I make myself comfortable, putting my feet up on the coffee table and hoping belatedly they don't stink too much. I lean forward to take a discreet sniff, and I think I'm in the clear. Leaning my head back against the couch cushions, I let out a breath. It's such a relief not to have to sit in the car for a fucking hour to get home. Sam plunks down on the far end of the couch, groaning as he puts his feet on the table beside mine.

"Oh, fuck me, that feels good," he says, wiggling his toes and grinning. "Mason just texted me back. Of course, he wants you to let them know if you need anything or if anything in the house starts acting weird because of the storm. I've been instructed to 'fucking behave myself.'" A laugh erupts from his chest, and my heart gives a little flutter. Sam laughs a lot, and when he does, he throws his head back and just lets go, the joyful sound coming straight from his belly, like his entire body is laughing. It's contagious, and I let out a chuckle of my own.

We're quiet for a moment, unwinding. The wind must be insanely strong because my aids are picking up the occasional cracking and groaning of the big trees outside, and the house shudders just slightly with each strong gust. We're sitting there, enjoying the small pleasures of being warm and dry inside during a storm, when a god-awful cracking sound comes in loud and clear, causing us both to jump. It literally sounds like a tree is about to fall on the house, and Sam and I look at each other wide-eyed. As we jump to our feet, we hear a giant thud that sounds like someone dropped a fucking elephant right outside, and the house shakes like it's about to come right off its foundation. At the exact same moment, we're plunged into total darkness as the power cuts out.

"Holy shit," Sam shouts, and he fumbles to hit the light on his phone. We slowly make our way to the window facing out to the driveway, and thankfully, they must have battery-operated emergency lights that have kicked on outside. They provide just enough light for us to see that one of the towering trees lining the long driveway has come down. It's fucking huge, and I don't know how it missed this building because it's literally right beside us. But thank fuck, it didn't hit either this place or the main house. Its giant trunk is lying across the driveway, blocking in Sam's truck and any other cars Mason and Jax might have parked in their garage. Looks like no one is going anywhere tonight.

CHAPTER 6

SAM

"Holy fucking fuck!" I say as we stand at the window, staring down at the driveway. I can see the look of shock on Tyler's face as he takes in the scene spread out below us. The wind and rain are still coming down, and the limbs of the trees are waving wildly. The emergency outdoor lights are just bright enough to see the ground is covered in smaller branches, tree limbs, and other assorted chunks of vegetation that have blown off. I'm shocked by the size of the tree that came down. And I'm thanking the universe that it fell in the direction of the driveway instead of into this building because I'm fairly certain we would have been goners. As it is, aside from trapping me and everyone else at Mason and Jax's place until we can get it removed, it doesn't appear to have caused much damage.

I unlock my phone and text Mason and Jackson, letting them know we're safe and not to come outside to check on us. This property is so heavily treed that going outside right now isn't safe, as evidenced by the massive evergreen tree currently blocking the driveway. Within seconds, Mason texts back.

> *Mason: Fuck, thank god it fell that way. We couldn't tell and I was about to go out and check. Jax was freaking out.*

> *Sam: well, see, there are these things we call phones now, and you can use them to contact people without having to physically go to be with them. It's super helpful if getting to where they are is difficult.*

> *Mason: eye roll emoji. Fine, asshole. Maybe I DO wish the fucking tree hit the guesthouse.*

Me: Grinning emoji

Me: You love me. But all is fine. Safe and sound other than being without power everything's normal. Unless something weird happens, we'll see you in the morning.

Mason: Sounds good. Like I said earlier. Fucking behave yourself. There are emergency candles in one of the kitchen drawers.

"Okay," I say to Tyler. "Mason was about to come check on us, but I told them to stay put since it's still blowing like hell out there, and it looks like any damage is minor. That was wild." I'm a little shaky as the adrenaline that surged through me moments ago starts to fade.

"Yeah. It really was," Tyler says with a tight smile. I can't tell for sure in the low light, but he looks a little pale. I know he struggled with

PTSD for a while. I hope this storm hasn't triggered some bad memories for him.

"Are you up for finishing your beer? Maybe we'll be able to get our heart rates under control." I laugh, and then it occurs to me that my plan to head home after one drink isn't going to happen. We're both here for the night, apparently. In a one-bedroom guest flat. With the power out and a vicious storm raging outside. Having narrowly escaped death by the skin of our teeth as a giant tree fell only a few feet from us. I grab my beer off the table and gulp down a couple of big swallows, feeling like I'm in the plot of some kind of romance—or maybe murder novel.

"Mason said there are some candles in the kitchen," I say, using my phone's light to navigate over to the drawer, where I grab a couple, together with a lighter and two more beers from the fridge.

After setting up the candles on the coffee table in front of us, I grab a cozy blanket from the basket beside the fireplace, tossing one corner of it to Tyler while I settle myself in the opposite corner. I'm still off-kilter from the adrenaline, and I'm betting he probably is as well.

We sit quietly for a few moments. I listen to the storm outside, concerned about other trees falling, but it sounds like the wind might be dying down, so maybe we'll escape death after all. Tyler is quiet, but his hand shakes when he goes to take a sip from his beer.

"Tyler, are you—is everything okay?" I ask hesitantly. I don't want to offend him, but he really doesn't look okay.

He lets out a shaky breath, and I think he's going to brush me off, but then he meets my eyes and shivers visibly.

"I'm, um. It. The tree was so loud. And the building shaking. It brought back some bad memories." He looks down, like he's embarrassed. "You'd think I'd be happy to be able to hear something loud and clear like that." He leans forward, setting his beer on the table and resting his elbows on his knees. He pinches the bridge of his nose with his hand still shaking.

I watch him for a second, and he looks so stressed-out it's like he might break. *Fuck it.* I slide closer to him on the couch, wrapping my arms around him and pulling him close to me. He stiffens at first, but a moment later, he leans in and wraps his arms around my waist, holding on for dear life.

CHAPTER 7

TYLER

How Sam figured out I needed to be held, I have no idea, but until he slid over and grabbed me, I felt like I was about to break apart at the seams. The sound and vibration of the giant tree falling triggered something. It's not an actual flashback—I haven't lost touch with reality. I know where I am and that I'm safe. I just feel weird. Unmoored or disoriented or something. The way Sam's arms are wrapped around me, firm but not restrictive, must be releasing some kind of chemical or hormone because I can feel my body beginning to slow down.

I lean against his broad chest and swallow the lump in my throat, still holding on to him for dear life. He traces his fingers gently over the back of my neck, leaving his other arm wrapped around me.

His breath ghosts against the shell of my ear, and I think he's murmuring things to me, although I can't hear them; I can only feel soft vibrations moving through his chest as he talks and feel his warm breath on my skin. It takes a while, but slowly, my body starts to re-regulate, my breathing slowing to at least a semblance of normal and my heart rate coming back down.

We've somehow shifted so I'm basically sitting on Sam's lap. And I'm suddenly very aware that underneath my hip, Sam's dick is as hard as steel.

Oh, fuck.

I shift slightly, putting more direct but subtle pressure on him, and his breath catches. My cock starts to fill immediately, and I slide one of my hands from his back to his chest, grasping onto his shirt and nuzzling into him.

Sam's heart is racing under my cheek, and I move my head so I can place my mouth on his neck, kissing him softly and smiling to myself as I feel his breath catch again, and the vibration of a moan moves through his chest.

Suddenly, I'm seized with a boldness that's totally unlike me, and before I even think, I've shifted so I'm straddling him, my hands on his shoulders. He slides his hands down to my ass, pulling me closer to him still, and we look into each other's eyes for just a second before I lean forward and take his mouth with mine.

Holy shit. His lips are velvety soft but firm. I trace the seam with my tongue, and he opens for me, shuddering as I feel him groan. There's an explosion of hot lava low down in my belly, and I shift my hips against him so our rock-hard cocks are pressed together, and it's my turn to let out a moan. I dip my tongue into his mouth, tasting and exploring him gently, moving my hands from his shoulders to the sides of his face so I can hold him exactly where I want him. We kiss for what seems like hours; somehow, neither one of us is in a hurry to do anything else. And dear god, the man knows how to kiss.

We trade dominance several times, first with me leading the way, then pulling back so Sam is the one in charge for long moments, exploring me with his tongue and his hands, before I take the lead again.

I can't help myself, and I grind my hips against him, rolling them in delicious circles as he bucks into me, seeking the pressure and friction. "Oh, fuck, Tyler," he says when I pull my mouth off his so I can trace the cords of his neck with my tongue.

His body is warm and strong underneath me, and all I can think about is touching his skin, so I slide my hands down to his waistband and up under his shirt. His back is smooth and velvety soft, his muscles strong and hard beneath his skin.

Both our movements become more deliberate, and it's not long before we're rutting against each other like a couple of animals. It feels incredible.

A thin sheen of sweat has broken out on his forehead as we strain and grind into each other, each chasing our release. Sam's head falls back against the couch as all his muscles tense, and he lets out a cry overflowing with passion, and it pulls me closer to the edge. As I reach the peak, I bite down on his bottom lip, and I feel rather than hear him moan again, his cock jerking against mine through our jeans.

"Oh fuck, oh fuck, oh fuck, I'm coming," I whisper harshly as I fall over the edge, squeezing my eyes tightly shut as the orgasm rips through me. I come and come and come for what feels like forever until I'm spent, and the only thing I can do is collapse against him, boneless and exhausted.

CHAPTER 8

SAM

Blinking slowly, I crack one eye open to figure out where I am. I'm boiling hot because something heavy and warm is on top of me and—ohhh. Right. Tyler. He's draped over me, his head resting on my chest and one arm thrown across my midsection, our legs tangled together. We're snuggled into the soft, deep couch in Mason and Jackson's guesthouse. Last night's events rush back to me, and suddenly, I'm very much awake.

Holy hell, I fooled around with Tyler. I've always thought he was hot as fuck, but he's way younger than me, and besides that, he's an employee. This is not a good thing. My brain is telling me to jump up and get the hell out of there as fast as possible, but I can't bring myself to disturb him. He looks so peaceful sleeping with his head resting on my chest. Tightness spreads through my belly. It felt incredible being with him that way. I've dated a lot of people, men and women, and I don't think anyone has ever made me come as hard as Tyler did last night. And it was just a make-out session with a little frotting. My breath catches as I imagine what it would feel like to be with him for real. Skin on skin, nothing between us... *Fucking hell. I cannot let myself go down this road.* If I'm not careful, I'll find myself hopelessly infatuated with Tyler, as I usually do, which cannot happen. Especially if I don't want my cousins to murder me. If I screw this up and it leads to Tyler quitting, Mason and Dylan will have my balls in a vise. *Shit, shit, shit.*

Tyler stirs and stretches against me like a cat, and god, it feels nice. If I stop myself from flipping out for two seconds, I can appreciate how good it is to wake up with someone curled up beside me.

I didn't intend to make a pass at him when I tried to comfort him last night, but he seemed like he needed a hug so damn badly. He looked so alone and stressed-out. And when he started kissing me, it was like a dam broke, and all I could do was hold on for the ride. I've always thought Tyler was gorgeous and sweet as hell, but when I tried getting to know him when he first started working with us, he shut me down, so I backed off. He's a lot more relaxed now, but we still don't know each other well.

"Mmmm," he moans softly as he slowly blinks his eyes open. Confusion flashes over his face at first, and then it's like everything comes rushing back to him the same way it did for me.

"Oh! Oh… Oh!" he exclaims, pushing back from me awkwardly, trying to untangle himself as fast as possible. He's a little too quick on the draw, losing his balance and tumbling off the edge of the couch, his ass hitting the floor with a loud thud. He looks up at me with wide eyes, and we both crack up.

"Um… hi!" I chuckle.

"Hi!" he says back, scrambling to his feet.

"So. Uh… did you sleep okay?" I ask awkwardly. I'm not unfamiliar with hookup etiquette, but I've never done it with someone I work with. Someone I see on an almost daily basis. *Fucking hell.*

He blinks at me and shakes his head, reaching to grab something off the coffee table. He fusses with one of his ears, and I realize he didn't have his hearing aids in, so he probably didn't hear my question.

He flashes a cute smile. "Sorry, I didn't have my ears in yet. Uh, what did you say?"

"Just wondered if you slept okay?" I ask, clearing my throat and getting up off the couch so I'm standing beside him. I automatically reach out to start straightening the pillows and folding the blanket, trying to avoid looking him in the eye.

"Yeah. I, um, I actually slept really good." He clears his own throat. "You?"

"Um, yeah, me too," I say, turning to put the blanket back in the basket it came from. We're both fully clothed, and I vaguely remember a bleary-eyed trip to the bathroom to clean myself up after coming in my pants like a fourteen-year-old. I ditched my cum-covered boxers, so I'm going commando under my jeans.

"Um, I'm just going to, uh, clean up a little," he says before scurrying off toward the bathroom. I breathe a sigh of relief. I think we both need a minute to process. Hopefully once we're fully awake, some of this awkwardness will disappear.

Tyler comes back a few minutes later as I'm standing in the kitchen, filling the coffeepot with water. By some miracle, the power is already back on, so I'm wasting no time getting caffeine into our systems. It's still early, and the sun isn't fully up yet, but there's a little bit of watery, gray light coming in through the windows. I don't hear the wind blowing or the trees creaking and cracking anymore, so it looks like the storm blew itself out. I finish setting up the coffee and walk over to the window to check out the damage. Sure enough, the giant fir tree is lying across the driveway, only about three feet clear of my truck's back bumper. Small mercies, I guess. At least we won't have to worry about insurance claims for a wrecked truck.

I know Mason and Jackson are probably going to be here as soon as they wake up, likely anxious to check out the damage from the tree and make sure there aren't any other big concerns.

Tyler comes to stand beside me at the window a moment later. "Wow. That's a really big fucking tree!" he remarks, and I chuckle.

"Yeah, sure is. God, we are so damn lucky it didn't hit the house. Or the truck."

"No kidding," he says.

The single-cup coffee maker beeps to signal it's ready, so I head back into the kitchen.

"Coffee?" I ask Tyler, but he shakes his head.

"Um... no, I'm okay. I think I'm probably just going to call an Uber and head back to my car. I should try to get home early today."

"Oh, sure. Right," I say, and I don't know why a stab of disappointment slices through my gut. I should be happy he's going to take off. My cousin and his husband are going to be here any minute, and their questions are going to be intense, especially if we're both here and acting super awkward. So why is it bugging me that Tyler clearly wants to get out of here as fast as humanly possible?

He whips out his phone and claims the closest rideshare. "Looks like it will be here in eight minutes," he says, and I force a smile.

"Great. You're smart to get out of here before Mason and Jax wake up. They're going to be ruthless with their questions." I mean it as a tease, but I immediately feel bad when his eyes get wide, and a worried look appears on his face.

"Oh, is it—will Mason be mad? I mean—"

I cut him off with a wave of my hand. "No, it's fine, Tyler. Don't worry about it. I'm just teasing. Mason won't give us a hard time. We're adults—what we do on our own time isn't his business. He'll be fine," I say, wishing I believed it. I know Mason won't be pissed off at Tyler, but he might give me that look he gets when he's worried about me.

"Um, anyway, I'm going to head out to wait for my ride," Tyler says, turning to head for the door.

Once he's got his shoes and coat on, there's a weird, awkward moment where neither of us knows how we're supposed to say goodbye. Like, what's our relationship now? Was that just a hookup? Something more? Would Tyler even want anything more with me? Jesus Christ, this is complicated. I don't know how this is going to work, but we need to figure it out.

Tyler clears his throat uncomfortably. "Uh, okay, then. Uh. I'll see you on Monday, I guess," he says, giving me a weird half wave.

"Yeah, no worries," I say with forced cheerfulness. I cock an eyebrow at him, and then to my horror, I click my tongue and give him the finger-gun gesture. "You drive safe now, young man!" I say with a wink. And never in my life have I wanted the floor to open up and swallow me more than at this very moment. *Finger guns? Really, Sam? Jesus Christ.*

Tyler gives me a strange look. "Uh, yeah, thanks," he says before turning and heading out the door.

His footsteps fade after he gets to the bottom of the stairs, and I lean forward with my elbows on the counter, holding my head in my hands. *Goddamn it. What have I done?*

CHAPTER 9

TYLER

After I make it home Saturday morning, the rest of the weekend goes by in the blink of an eye, I've been completely tied up in knots since Friday night's... adventures and Saturday morning's horrifying "walk of shame" routine.

I don't know what to think. Sam is hot. Like smokeshow hot, and he's an amazing person. I know this from watching him over the past few years. He's such a great person that there's no possible way he could be interested in me, other than as a friend or work acquaintance. That probably explains why he was acting so weird on Saturday morning.

Since my energy was mostly wrapped up in worrying about the situation with Sam, I didn't spend much time worrying about the whole "moving to the coast for several months" thing. Mason would like me to volunteer for the role, but I don't know what to do. I mean, I'd be stupid not to jump at the chance, right? But when I think about it, my stomach clenches with nerves.

For most people, getting an opportunity like this would be like winning the lottery. I've known for a while that I need to get out of my tiny, crappy apartment in the nasty part of town, but the thought of going through the whole process of looking for a place, trying to communicate with a new landlord, moving all my stuff and dealing with all the other million things moving would require makes me break out in hives. Even before losing my hearing, it would have been an ordeal, but throw communication difficulties into the mix and I dread it. If I had to do it for my job, it would be a way to force myself into it. I could give up my apartment for a few months, and when the job at the coast ended, I could just find a new place closer to Seattle.

I'm pretty sure I can handle the job, but the thought of having to manage people makes me crazy anxious. I've been able to carve out a little comfort zone at work for the past couple of years. Everyone knows me, and I don't have to worry about people acting weird or that I'll miss anything important. People know all the little things they can do to help me communicate with them more easily. But maybe it's time to stretch myself a little bit. This is a great job with a great company and amazing people. I'll never find a better working situation. It's probably the safest place I'll ever find to try and get out of my comfort zone.

Working in construction was never what I had planned, although sometimes plans change. Mostly I've accepted it, although every so often, my old dream of being an art teacher pops into my head. Mostly when I'm alone with my sketchpad somewhere. But I always tamp those thoughts down. I'm sure there are deaf teachers out there, but the thought of trying to keep control of a class full of rowdy teenagers when I can't properly hear what's going on around me makes me shudder. I'd feel like I was missing things that went on in the classroom. I mean, nothing is impossible, but I just don't know whether I'm cut out for it anymore.

Because I don't have anything else to dis-tract me, my mind wanders over to its favorite spot—the guilt section. I had loosely planned to visit my mom in the care home this weekend, but after getting home on Saturday, still tied up in knots over the hookup with Sam—or whatever it was—I just couldn't face it. Couldn't face her. I tried to convince myself I didn't go because the roads were still in rough shape after the storm, with lots of debris down and traffic lights out. But that's not the real reason. I dread visiting her at the best of times, and when I'm stressed-out, it's even worse. Not that she'll notice or care. She almost never recognizes me anymore. I also understand intellectually that I don't owe her anything. My guilt doesn't make her life any better, and it sure as fuck doesn't help me. It also doesn't change the fact that she was a shitty mother, and I had a really shitty childhood.

My brother, Aaron, visits her more than I do, and that's yet another source of guilt. Thinking about Aaron ramps up my guilt to astronomical levels. Even before dementia took over her brain, my mother spent most of her time in a drunken haze. I'm pretty sure there were times she didn't remember she even had kids. She certainly never cared enough to make us a priority in her life. Aaron, on the other hand, was one of the only people who gave half a shit about me, and our relationship is currently circling the drain.

I didn't know how to behave when I first came back from overseas, and one night, we had a terrible argument. It never got physical, but we both said things that are hard to take back. I understand where he was coming from now, after many hours of talking with my therapist. Hurt and anger will make you say shit you truly don't mean. But neither one of us has been able to figure out how to get past the horrible things we said to each other. Even with all my therapy, I still can't see a way to make things right with the most important person in my life. It eats at me.

Thankfully, the traffic picks up, so I don't have a lot of time to work myself into a guilty, anxious mess. Or at least no more a mess than usual.

After pulling up to the office, I pause to stretch as I get out of my little Honda. Because I was running late this morning, I had no chance to make coffee at home, so my sole focus is on getting caffeine into my system, stat, as I head toward the kitchen. Still lost in thoughts of my mother and Aaron, I crash directly into someone as I step into the kitchen. Looking up, I find Sam's big, brown eyes staring down at me, a hint of amusement crinkling the corners as he gives me a crooked grin that makes my stomach do a flip-flop.

"Whoa, there!" he says, jumping back.

"Oh, hey, Sam," I say. And then it's like we both remember what happened on Friday night, and a bucket of ice-cold awkward gets dumped all over us. He looks down at his feet like the secrets of the universe are painted on his work boots. Clearing his throat, he glances at me briefly before returning his eyes to his feet. "Uh. Did you have a good rest of the weekend?" he asks politely, and I nod, cringing internally.

"Yeah, it was fine," I say with a forced smile. "Sorry I crashed into you; I wasn't paying attention."

"Oh, yeah, that's, uh... no problem." Oh god, this might be the most awkward situation I've ever experienced, even worse than Saturday morning. I'm desperate to escape, but he's blocking the door to the kitchen with his broad shoulders. It would look weird if I suddenly turned around and headed for my desk. Sam clears his throat again, and the heat coming off my cheeks could probably power a small city.

"Um, right. I should... yeah, better get to work..." he says in a weird, fake-cheery tone.

"Right," I say, stepping to the side to get out of his way. He steps the same way, and it results in us trying to dodge each other in what looks like some kind of weird two-step.

Finally, we manage to break free of the dance routine, and he chuckles nervously. "Sorry 'bout that... I'm just going to... um—yeah. Back to work." He walks away, and I let out the breath I didn't realize I was holding.

I make my way over to the fancy-ass Nespresso machine Jackson bought for us. None of us are really fancy coffee drinkers, but Jax is a sweetheart, and he thought it would be nice for us on the cold winter days, especially if we're heading to or coming back from an outdoor worksite.

I'm waiting for the coffee when a big, warm paw lands on my shoulder. I jump, turning to see Mason standing beside me.

"Hey, good morning," he says, reaching for a mug. "How was the rest of your weekend?" We make small talk for a few minutes while the machine hisses and gurgles its way to coffee perfection. We're walking out of the kitchen when he says casually, "Would you drop by my office to chat for a minute once you've got yourself settled?"

I swallow so loud I'm sure he can hear it. I know he's going to ask me to take the job in Ocean Shores.

"Oh sure, yeah, just give me a few minutes."

I drop my bag at my desk and head down the hallway to where Mason and Dylan have side-by-side offices looking out onto the forest behind the office.

Mason is sitting at his desk, staring at his laptop screen when I walk in. He gives me a huge smile. "Hey, Tyler, come on in and have a seat."

I swallow nervously as I take the seat across from him. I still don't know whether I'm ready for this job. It's a lot of responsibility.

"Hey, man, I know you have a jobsite to get to, so I'll get right to the point. I want to officially ask you if you'd be interested in taking the job out in Ocean Shores," he says. Even though I was expecting it, I'm still a little shocked when the words come out of his mouth.

"Naturally, your salary will be adjusted to reflect your new responsibilities." Mason slides a piece of paper across the desk with some numbers scrawled on it, including my current salary info. But my eyes nearly fall out of my head at the new salary he's proposing.

"Holy shit!" I say and then clap my hand over my mouth, sucking in air between my fingers. "Sorry!" I blurt. "Wow, I, um... just wow. I wasn't expecting this," I say, stunned at the number on the paper in front of me.

Mason's smiling broadly. "Truth is, Tyler, you've been due for a raise and a promotion for a while, but we weren't in a position to offer it to you until we had this job and a couple of other big ones locked down. Hot Dam Homes has had great success over the last couple of years, and you've been a huge part of it. We want to show how much we appreciate your work, and this salary is more appropriate for what we want you to do. And we're more than confident you can handle it."

I sit there, dumbfounded, not sure what to say.

"Sam has agreed to take the other long-term position. Since it's such a big job, I see you two working as partners. I know you guys will make a great team, and you'll be able to learn a ton from him."

I snap my gaze over to him, wondering whether he knows what happened between Sam and me on Friday night. I can't tell from the look on his face, but if he knows anything, he's not saying.

"It probably feels overwhelming, but I promise, no one's throwing you out there to sink or swim." He smiles. "Sam will be there to help you along, not as your manager but more like a senior partner. There's just one thing though. You guys will need to be roommates if you want HDH to cover your housing costs. The property owner tells me there's a guest cabin on-site that was recently renovated. I haven't seen it, but he assures me it's big enough for two guys to live in. I know you're not big on the idea of roommates, but Sam's easy to live with. He and I were roommates a long time ago, and it worked great." Mason looks nervous, like this might be a deal breaker for me.

"Oh, um, that... I think that will work fine," I say, still mostly focused on the paper detailing my new salary.

"Okay, good. Hang on a sec, I'm going to bring Sam in so we can chat about the logistics for a minute," he says, grabbing his cell phone to send a text.

A minute later, Sam comes into the office, and he's smiling, but I can see the tension lurking underneath.

He takes the seat beside me, and when I glance at him, he's cracking his knuckles and nibbling on his bottom lip. My mind conjures up the feeling of him biting down hard on my lip the other night, how the pleasure mixed with a little pain was so fucking hot. I want him to be chewing on my lip instead of his own. *Fuck, Tyler. Focus. Now is not the time.*

"So, congratulations, you guys!" Mason grins, and then he gets a funny look on his face. "Wait, I just realized Tyler hasn't even officially agreed to this whole idea. I'm so sorry, Tyler! I don't want to pressure you if you need some time to think about it." He looks slightly embarrassed.

I shake my head. "I'd be crazy not to say yes to all this. It's a great opportunity. I'll take the job," I say, and Mason's expression changes to delight, a big smile stretching across his face.

"Yeah? That's what I was hoping you'd say." He extends a hand across his desk, and I stand, shaking it awkwardly.

"I'm really glad you want to do this for us, with us," he says, and I glance over at Sam, who's also beaming at me, seemingly having pushed away his own nerves.

We chat for a few minutes about some of the details, but I don't think I'll be able to remember a damn thing, my mind swirling with thoughts about how my life is about to change and all the things I'm going to have to do to get ready for this.

"Okay, you two. I'll let you work out the rest of the details together, but let's talk tomorrow," Mason finishes. "And thank you both again for taking this on. I think it's going to be great!"

Before I realize what's happening, Mason comes around the desk and wraps his huge arms around me in a tight hug.

I hug him back, trying desperately to swallow back the lump that has suddenly materialized in my throat.

"You've really earned this, you know," he says, pulling back so I can see his face but keeping his hands on my shoulders. "You're a valuable asset to this company, and I want to keep you around for as long as possible. I hope it doesn't sound condescending, Ty, but I'm proud of you. You've grown a lot since you started here."

No one has ever told me they were proud of me, and it hits me right in the chest. For a moment, I'm too choked up to speak.

"You're gonna be great at this job, I know it," he says, rescuing me from having to say anything. "I'm sure you're going to have a million questions the second you walk out of here, so come talk to me or text me anytime. But let's plan for you guys to be there in about two weeks, okay?"

"Right, okay, great, thank you. Thanks a lot, Mason." I practically trip over my own feet as I race out of his office. I need a few minutes alone to process.

I'm still reeling when Sam pokes his head around the wall of my cubicle a couple of minutes later. I didn't even make it as far as my own chair—I've just flopped down in one of the two chairs on the opposite side of the desk, staring at the paper with my new job details on it.

"You okay?" he asks.

"Yeah, yeah, I'm good. I'm fine. I'm just surprised. I suspected he was going to ask me to go to Ocean Shores, but this promotion and the raise..." I shake my head. "Fuck, Sam, I just... I hope I'm up for it."

His eyes soften, and he walks into my cubicle, sliding into the chair beside me.

"You're totally up for it, Tyler. You're going to be great."

"Thanks. I just... It's a lot of responsibility."

The smile he gives me is full of something I can't read. Tenderness, fondness... maybe even pride. "They all see the same thing I do, that you're great at this job and you're a phenomenal person." Our eyes lock, and a stab of longing pierces my gut so strongly I almost jump. Sam clears his throat uncomfortably and then lowers his voice, so I need to watch his mouth carefully to understand him. I can't stop looking at his mouth and remembering what it feels like against my skin, and my mouth goes suddenly dry.

"So, um... I want to make sure you're okay with us being there together. After Friday, I mean. I don't want you to feel... obligated... or anything." We've both shifted forward in our chairs, and his face is so close to mine his breath ghosts across my cheek. His eyes have darkened, his pupils blown out, making him look sexy as fuck.

"Oh! No, that's... It's no problem," I stutter, feeling about as smooth as a cactus in a silk robe. "I'm—I know it's not—" I force myself to stop and take a breath. "Thanks for saying that, but I know it won't be an issue. We're both adults, right? We didn't really plan for what happened on Friday. I mean, things happen, right?"

He nods. "Yeah, okay. Well, um, if anything changes and you don't feel comfortable, you can let me or Mason know. I mean, I haven't told him about what happened, but you can... if you want. But..." Now it's Sam's turn to stumble over his words, and I laugh. For some reason, his nervousness gives me confidence it will work out somehow.

"Don't worry, Sam. It's okay. It will be fine."

"Okay. Okay..." he says, giving me a cautious look like he wants to double-check I am, in fact, fine with the situation. "Right, then. Um. Okay, I'll just get out of your way, then."

He gives me a slightly awkward wave before rushing out of my cubicle, and I'm left wondering if I'm having a similar effect on him as he's having on me.

And now we're going to be roommates for months at some isolated resort in the middle of nowhere? Motherfucker.

CHAPTER 10

TYLER

The next two weeks fly by. I make all the arrangements I need to, giving notice on my apartment and canceling all the services like internet and utilities. Even though I've been delaying, I feel good knowing I'll be getting out of this crappy apartment in the even crappier neighborhood. With my raise and the money I'll save while I don't have to pay rent, I'll be able to afford a way better place. Fuck, maybe I'll even be able to find something where I don't have to haul my fucking laundry down five flights of stairs—maybe even something with a functioning dryer. I'll be living like a king, I snicker to myself as I grab my still-damp clothes from the various random places I hung them in the hopes they might dry before Sam comes to get me.

When he offered to drive us both out to Ocean Shores, I figured it was a good idea, especially since Mason let me store my car at his place. What I hadn't thought about until last night was that if Sam picked me up, he was going to see where I live. It's not exactly a desirable neighborhood. It's alarmingly close to what's basically an open-air drug market a few blocks away, and the rest of the street is lined with pawn shops, bail bondsmen, and gun stores. Not exactly the kind of place they're putting on tourist brochures, but I grew up not far from here, and even though it's a tough neighborhood, it's familiar. I'm self-conscious about it though, especially with someone like Sam, who grew up in a comfortable, middle-class home. Combine that with my anxiety around the new job and nerves about having Sam as a roommate, and I didn't sleep much last night. That, of course, only makes things worse since not sleeping well can bring on my nightmares, and if there is one thing I don't want Sam to see, it's one of my nightmares.

I don't know why, but I just couldn't muster up the courage to ask about the specific set-up of our temporary home. Will we have our own rooms, or are we sharing? What about the kitchen and living area situation? If we're sharing a room, what happens when he wants to stay up late and I need to stick to my early bedtime routine? I don't want to force anyone to live on my hours. The thought of explaining why I was so concerned about these details was too much, so instead, I just stewed silently. Definitely the most responsible choice. *Fuck. My. Life.*

When Sam texts he's out front, I take one last look around the dumpy little place and walk out without regret. The building manager is going to get rid of the little furniture I had, and I rented a small storage locker for the few things I want to keep. The rest of my stuff is packed up to come with me, and it all fits into a smallish duffel bag, a small suitcase, and my toolbox. I'm not sure whether having this tiny number of possessions is something to be proud of or ashamed of.

My biggest worry is that I'm going to embarrass the fuck out of myself by having a nightmare in front of Sam. There have been times, when the nightmares have been particularly bad, that I've wet the bed and/or puked all over the place. The thought of having that happen in front of a coworker, and even worse, someone I'm attracted to, is enough to make me reconsider taking the job in the first place.

I get downstairs with my stuff to find Sam waiting by the open tailgate of the truck. He has everything neatly packed and covered with a tarp to protect it from the rain that will almost certainly be falling today, being winter in the PNW.

"Anything else need to come down?" he asks after we've packed my things.

"Nope," I reply.

"Really? You're not bringing much. You know we're gonna be there for a few months, right?" He bumps his shoulder against mine to show he's teasing, and I force a smile.

"Nah, I travel light. Military habits die hard, I guess."

"Okay, then." He grins, slamming the tailgate shut. "Alright. First order of business: snacks."

"What, why? It's only a couple of hours, isn't it?" I ask while sliding into the passenger seat.

Sam looks at me, his eyes wide with shock. "Dude, come on! If you don't pack road trip snacks like an unsupervised kid with $100 in a gas station, you're doing it wrong."

I roll my eyes and chuckle. Sam really is such a dad at heart.

So we stop for gas and snacks before getting on the Interstate, and true to his word, Sam loads up with candy as if he's that unsupervised kid he was talking about.

Once we've been driving for a while, the silence starts to feel uncomfortable. We haven't spoken about our hookup the night of the storm, and I don't know how to bring it up. Honestly, I don't know how to feel about it, but I do know a large part of me really wants it to happen again. We can't though. I know we can't. Hooking up with a coworker is never a good plan, and I don't do relationships anyway. I'm way too fucked-up to ask another person to take on my shit.

We get to Olympia area around lunchtime, and Sam reaches over and squeezes my knee to get my attention. I startle as the warmth of his hand causes little zings of electricity to travel up my thighs right to my balls. *God, this man.* No one has ever affected me physically like the way Sam does.

"Hey, do you want to stop and grab lunch somewhere?" he asks.

"Yeah, I could eat," I say.

We stop at a little dive bar, and the waitress gives us a nod with her chin to seat ourselves, so we settle into a booth. When she comes to the table, I order a Coke, and Sam orders a beer. He seems nervous and jumpy, same as me, and after a few miserable attempts at small talk, we just sit there, marinating in awkward sauce.

"So," he says, and I get the feeling he's desperately grasping at anything to make conversation at this point. It's not surprising, since I'm not giving him any help. He probably thinks my silent treatment means I'm pissed at him instead of the reality: I'm stewing in my own neurosis. *Social anxiety and PTSD FTW.*

He clears his throat. "So, you grew up around here, right? Have you been out this way before? To the coast, I mean?"

"Nope," I say, shaking my head and taking a drink of my Coke.

"Oh. My family used to go out to the Oregon Coast every year. I used to love hanging out with all my cousins and playing on the beach all summer." He smiles. "Every Fourth of July, we'd have a huge fireworks display on the beach, even though it was technically not allowed, and we'd have beach bonfires nearly every night."

"Yeah, well, not every family is the kind who takes happy vacations and jaunts to the beach every year. My family sure as hell wasn't," I say shortly and immediately feel like shit at the way he recoils like I've smacked him. *What in the hell is wrong with me?* Sam wasn't taunting me or trying to point out that he had a better childhood than me. But I'm so nervous and sleep deprived, I'm irritable as fuck. I know Derek would tell me Sam's trying to get to know me, and my anxiety is trying to pull me back, away from this new experience that my brain perceives as dangerous.

"Oh, I'm sorry. I didn't mean to make you uncomfortable," Sam sputters, color rising on his cheeks. I feel even more like an asshole.

"Oh, fuck, Sam, I'm sorry," I blurt out.

He nods without looking me in the eyes and takes a sip from his beer. "It's okay," he says quietly. The rest of lunch crawls by at a glacial pace while I stew about what an idiot I am and how badly I'm fucking everything up. By the time we walk back out to the truck, the tension between us is so thick I can almost taste it.

Once we're in the cab, I sigh heavily and lean forward on the seat, my elbows on my knees, holding my head in my hands. "Jesus fucking

Christ. I'm such an asshole," I mutter under my breath.

Keeping my eyes on the floor, I start talking. "I'm really sorry I snapped at you. I've, uh, been having some anxiety, and it's got the best of me today. I'm really sorry for acting like a dick." I look over at him to make sure I catch his response—assuming he has one.

He looks worried. "It's okay, Tyler. It just seems like you're really tense. What are you anxious about? Is it me? Being here with me? I don't want to make you uncomfortable. If you're not okay with rooming together, I'm sure we can figure something else out. Or I can talk to Mason and he can replace me with someone else. Or we could—" He's talking so fast I'm not getting every word, but I'm picking up on his worry loud and clear.

I shake my head emphatically, cutting him off. "No, no, no. It's not you, Sam. I'm sorry. I just... Fuck... You probably know I have PTSD, right?"

Sam nods, his eyes still concerned, but at least he's stopped gripping the steering wheel so hard his knuckles are white. "Yeah, Mason mentioned it back when you were first hired, just so we knew what kind of accommodations we needed to make. Is it going to be a problem for you? I know this place is a little isolated. Shit, I didn't even think to ask whether something might trigger you. I'm so sorry..."

"No, it's okay. One of my symptoms is nightmares. And I've had all this stuff about moving and this new job on my mind, and it's been affecting my sleep. When my sleep gets fucked-up, my anxiety gets worse, which makes me more likely to have nightmares." I sigh. "And my nightmares aren't fun for anyone. I don't want you to have to deal with me if I have one. I'm really sorry. I'm such a hot mess."

I let out a bitter-sounding laugh. This whole thing is so stupid. Sam is so earnest, trying so hard to make this easier for me, and I'm acting like a complete head case.

His face goes from concerned to puzzled as I laugh.

"Umm...?"

"It's not you, I promise. I'm a walking shitshow. My special power is fucking up any interpersonal relationship. My brother, friends, teachers, managers. My talent in this area is unparalleled." I'm still laughing, but I'm so frustrated I can barely stop myself from jumping out of the truck and running away in embarrassment.

He still looks concerned. "Oh. Are you... I mean... is there anything I can do to make things easier for you?"

I shake my head. "I just need to get over myself." I sigh. "I've been nervous about the sleeping arrangements because of the chance of nightmares. But of course, I was too nervous to ask anyone about it, so I just let it fester, which was clearly the best way to handle it," I say with a small smile that he returns cautiously.

"Well, I'm glad you told me it's a possibility," he says, his face relaxing a smidge. "If you do have a nightmare, is there anything I can do to help you?"

How is this guy even real?

"No, no, it's fine. If it happens, I'll handle it," I say dismissively, even though my stomach clenches, knowing that I don't "handle" my nightmares very well.

"Well, at least if something happens, I won't freak out and accidentally kill you with my ninja reflexes before I've fully woken up," he says with a totally straight face, and for a second, I can't tell if he's joking or not. But then I see him biting his lip, trying not to laugh as he takes in my confused expression, so I let out a chuckle.

"Oh. Is that something that's happened often?" I ask. "Like, have you accidentally killed people in the past with your lightning-fast ninja reflexes before you were awake?"

"Dude, come on. You know I can't talk about that kind of thing. If information like that were to get out, my cover as a secret ninja superhero would be completely blown."

"Right, sorry, I should have known." I shoot him a grin. "But I do feel better just knowing you won't turn your lethal ninja skills on me."

"I'm telling you—that's the best possible attitude. Just relax and let the ninja do his thing if he makes an appearance." He grins at me, and the tension hanging between us seems to disappear. The remainder of the drive is comfortable as we chat about everything and nothing, and I slowly begin to relax.

CHAPTER 11

SAM

After Tyler admits he's feeling anxious, the tension seems to dissipate. We still haven't talked about whatever is going on between us, but for now, it seems like we can shove it aside. Almost an hour after leaving the pub where we ate lunch, we turn onto the coastal highway that runs right along the edge of Washington State's rugged coastline. Ocean Shores is a tiny little town perched right on the edge of the continent. We spent many summers out here when I was a kid, but it's been a while since I've been here. I remember standing on these beaches, and my dad or my uncle Bob, Mason and Dylan's dad, would almost always point out to the horizon and say something like "you know, if you stepped into the water right here and just kept going, the next land you'd hit would be Japan." Mason and I would always roll our eyes when our dads would start talking like a couple of old sailors, but listening to those two get all philosophical are some of the best memories we have. It's heartbreaking to think that Tyler never had any of those experiences growing up. It sounds ridiculous, but part of me wants to give him those experiences now. It wouldn't be that hard. Just build a beach fire and roast some s'mores. It will be cold as fuck, but my chest does a funny, flippy thing when I think about how cool it would feel to show Tyler some of the best parts of my childhood.

I snort with laughter, and he shoots me a puzzled glance. "What?"

I shake my head. "Nothing, just having weird thoughts. It's been years since I've been back here. It's still pretty much how I remember it. I forgot how amazing this place is."

Tyler smiles and looks past me out the driver's-side window, watching the stunning waves lapping against the shore under the low, steely-gray clouds. I've always kind of thought of Tyler as a kid since he's so much younger than me, but looking at him now, I realize that even with our age difference, I'm probably more of a kid than he is. This man has been through some shit in his short life. From the little I know of him, Tyler's life wasn't exactly a fairy tale before he joined the army. His family sounds like it was kind of messed up, and coming back from Afghanistan with a life-changing injury hasn't made his life any easier.

A few minutes up the highway is the turnoff for the old resort. There's a long, winding drive through a border of thick evergreen trees before it opens up to a clearing. The old hotel buildings cling to the cliffside over the crashing waves below. The main building is long and narrow. It's a couple of stories tall, with rows of windows facing the water as the churning waves crash against the beach below. Its wood siding is bleached and faded from decades spent facing the harsh winds as violent winter storms roll in off the Pacific.

There are a couple of smaller buildings off to each side of the main one, and they look like they're in the same condition. Everything is worn and weathered and in need of a serious facelift, but it's easy to see the enormous potential here. This place could easily become a breathtaking, luxurious resort.

As we step out of the truck, the bitterly cold wind tries to steal the breath from my lungs. The ocean is wild and filled with whitecaps, and the trees have almost no branches on the side facing the water. Many of them are bent and curled in on themselves, so they look like people hunched over, trying to protect against the harsh weather. It's also loud. The ocean's roar provides constant background noise, but with the wind whipping past us, everything is heightened. Tyler looks at me and points to his ear. "I had to adjust the volume down because of the wind, so I won't be able to hear you until we're inside," he says.

I nod and take a few steps toward the water, taking in a deep lungful of the salty ocean air. There's an old wooden stairway zigzagging down the side of the cliff to the sand, and I can't wait to go down to the beach and explore. I wonder if things will be the way I remember.

I glance at Tyler to find him almost glowing. His eyes sparkle as he gazes out at the ocean, his cheeks already ruddy from the cold wind. He turns to me with a smile bright enough to light up the night sky. And holy fuck, do I ever want to be the one to put that smile on his face, again and again. I give him a grin and then gesture to the biggest building. "Let's check out the inside," I shout.

The inside is in better shape than the outside, but not by much. It has that damp, slightly musty smell that's impossible to escape when you're so close to the salt water. It's bone-chillingly freezing inside the building too, but there's a big stone fireplace taking up one wall.

"This will come in handy, especially early in the mornings or late in the evenings," I say over my shoulder, but Tyler's not facing me, and I don't think he's turned his hearing aids back on yet. He's standing by the huge picture window facing the water. His face is full of awe, and for a second, I just stare at him. The afternoon sunlight shines directly into the room, giving him a kind of ethereal glow, and a warm, soft feeling expands throughout my chest as I watch him experience this special place for the first time.

A few minutes later, he turns toward me, and when he realizes I've been staring at him, his ivory skin turns pink, and he fumbles with his hearing aids.

"Shit, I'm sorry, I forgot to turn them back on when we came inside. Were you talking to me?" he stammers.

"No, you're fine." I smile, trying to put him at ease. "You looked beautiful." Realizing what just came out of my mouth, it's my turn to start stammering awkwardly. "Um, uh—I mean, you looked like you were really appreciating the view. It's so beautiful," I say lamely, and he gives me a shy smile.

"It's really something," Tyler says and then turns to take in the rest of the big room. Mason said there have been a couple of attempts to renovate this place over the last decade, but for one reason or another, none of them got completed, so a lot of upgrades are started but not finished.

"I think this room is going to have a check-in desk up toward the front, but most of the space will be a gathering area for guests," I say before turning to head down the hallway.

"This place will be incredible once we're done with it, as long as the guy can afford to do it right," Tyler says, looking around.

I nod in agreement. "Yeah. From what Mason told me, the guy has pretty deep pockets. He's some big Hollywood producer or something. Sounds like he's back and forth to LA still, but he wants to retire here and run this place when he leaves California."

Reaching the end of the hallway, we climb the stairs to the second floor, which is lined on both sides with rooms. "We'll be taking down walls and combining them, so there will only be five or six luxury suites on this floor. I guess the owner wants every suite to have its own unique style."

Tyler's eyes grow wide. "Wow, Mason wasn't kidding when he said this would be a big job."

"Yeah, it's gonna be a fuck-ton of hard work, but I bet it's going to be sick when it's finished. And just think, Ty, one day, you'll be able to point to this fabulous, luxurious nest for the rich and famous and say you built that."

He grins, but I catch a glimpse of something sad flashing across his face before he can hide it. "Yea. Too bad I'll never be able to afford even a broom closet in a place like this."

I grin at him. "Neither will I, but it's sometimes about who you know, not how much money you have." I give him a wicked grin. "I've gotten to tag along on some amazing trips with Mason and Jax, because Jax has all these crazy connections to the ultra-rich and famous. You can never tell what might happen, you know? And I gotta tell you, I'm totally okay with being the 'poor relative' who sometimes gets to tag along on the private jet for vacations. I'll take those benefits without the stress of the high-pressure job!"

Tyler looks thoughtful. "Yeah, that's a good way to look at it," he says.

"Okay, then." I rub my hands together, trying to warm them up. "Let's head over to the guest-house. Mason didn't get a chance to check it out while he was here, since it's apparently already updated. The owner told him it's in good shape and should be fine to keep us warm and dry for the rest of the winter."

"Sure, let's go," Tyler responds, and we lock up the main building and head in the direction of the guest cabin.

CHAPTER 12

TYLER

I'd been kind of embarrassed when Sam caught me staring out the window, but I've never seen a view like that in real life. I'm dying to grab my sketchbook and charcoals, my hands itching to try to capture some of the wild, untamed beauty here. But I'll wait until we're finished with our tour of the property.

Weekends should be a good opportunity to do some drawing. It will be cold, but I'll be able to do some sketching and maybe try to get some good photos as well. I don't normally work in color, but I think I might try it with this landscape. I have to remind myself that I'm here to work, not play, and Sam gives me a friendly grin as we head back outside.

"I think the guest cabin is over this way," he says over his shoulder. I nod and follow him as he skirts around the truck and heads down a narrow path that cuts through the woods.

About fifty yards into the trees, he stops short, causing me to almost crash into him from behind. The building in front of us doesn't look much like a rustic cabin; it's more like a mini version of a luxury chalet. It's small, finished with cedar siding that's weathered to a silvery color. A pair of Adirondack chairs sits on a large porch, and the front door is painted red, the color faded from age and salt.

"Whoa. That's unexpected," Sam says. "I wonder if the inside is as nice as the outside." He unlocks the door, and we walk in to find a tiny but incredibly luxurious little space. The first floor is the main living area, with a kitchen to the right, a bathroom to the left, and a central room with a comfy-looking couch facing a stone fireplace, a flat-screen mounted above it. Big picture windows face out into the forest.

There's a loft area above, accessed by a narrow staircase that's more like a ladder than proper stairs. Since the building is surrounded by towering evergreen trees, we can't see the ocean through the windows, but I'm sure you can hear it if your ears work well enough.

The kitchen, while small, seems like something a gourmet chef would be happy with, and the bathroom looks like something out of a movie star's house, complete with multiple showerheads and a jetted soaker tub. We look at each other, our eyes wide with shock, but we both break into smiles at the same time. It's far nicer than expected. I mean, it's set up more like a romantic couples getaway spot instead a crash pad for a couple of construction workers, but hell, I'm not gonna complain. This is a level of luxury I could get used to.

"Dude, this place is fucking awesome!" Sam says, my hearing aids picking up the enthusiasm in his voice. "Let's go check out the bedrooms!"

His excitement is contagious, and I'm almost giddy as I follow him to the ladder leading upstairs. It takes Sam about three seconds to bound up it with me right behind him, but those three seconds give me a tantalizing view of his gorgeous ass. And for the second time, I nearly crash into him.

He stops once he gets to the top, blocking my way to get off the ladder thingy, so I lean over to see around him.

What we thought was two separate rooms up here, or at least an area with a couple of beds, turns out to be a large loft. There's a window on the back wall, and pushed right up against it is the biggest bed I've ever seen. It must be bigger than a king bed; maybe it's custom-made or something. But it's so huge that there's not a lot of floor space left.

"Oh!" I say in surprise.

We both stand still for a second, until the absurdity of the situation washes over me, and I burst into laughter.

CHAPTER 13

SAM

"Well, this is interesting." I say, staring at the giant bed taking up about 99 percent of the floor space up here. Tyler climbs up behind me, and he snorts as he takes in the huge bed. He pauses, looks around for a second, and then bursts into laughter.

"Well, at least it looks comfortable," he laughs.

Knowing he was already nervous about being roommates when we assumed there were a couple of bedrooms, or at least separate beds, I hope he isn't freaking out over the whole "only one bed" situation. But he seems to be genuinely amused, so I bark out a laugh of my own.

"Hmm. Good thing that couch looks comfy," I laugh. "Maybe we can figure out how to get this taken out and move a couple of smaller beds in here," I muse.

I glance over at Tyler, and he shrugs. "I'm smaller than you. I'll take the couch."

I roll my eyes since there is absolutely no way I'm letting him sleep on the couch. The guy is still carrying around pieces of shrapnel inside his body from the explosion he barely survived while he was serving our country. Hopefully Tyler doesn't try to argue with me.

"No way will you be the one sleeping on the couch, soldier." I hold up my hand when he starts to protest. "Let's go grab our bags. We'll worry about the sleeping arrangements later. I want to go into town to grab groceries since they probably close everything up early on Sundays," I say, and Tyler nods, turning to head back down the ladder.

· · • • • • • · ·

TYLER

We head into town and pick up enough supplies to last us the next few days at the tiny grocery store, and Sam insists on picking up some firewood. He gets all excited when he talks about having a beach fire and making s'mores, and it's completely adorable. I've never made s'mores over a campfire, and it sounds awesome. It's sweet how Sam seems to be trying to make this experience into something of a vacation for me. I would have thought it would make me defensive, which is typically my go-to reaction when I feel like the "poor kid" who never had the experiences or advantages most people take for granted growing up. But with Sam, for some reason, it's no big deal. He's clearly enjoying showing me around and explaining things about the area. My dick twitches in my jeans when he gets this confident, authoritative voice he uses when he's explaining things. Or when he's made a decision he will absolutely not back down from, like when he told me I wasn't allowed to sleep on the couch. A delicious little shiver rolls through me just thinking about it.

Even though I really try not to use alcohol as a crutch for my feelings, I'm thinking one or two beers right now might help settle me down a bit because this day has been kind of a wild ride. Between feeling vulnerable from my confession about my nightmares and then discovering we're going to be a lot cozier than we'd planned, I think I've earned a couple of drinks.

We get the groceries unloaded, and since it's a little too early to think about dinner, I decide I need some breathing space.

"Hey, I think I'm going to head down to the water and stretch my legs a bit," I say to Sam, who's kneeling in front of the gas fireplace, trying to get it turned on.

"Okay, cool," he says, sounding a little distracted.

I grab my sketchbook and tuck it under my arm as I head out the door. It's not like I hide my art from people, but I'm a little shy about showing it. Sketching and drawing calms my nerves. It helps me let go of stuff in my head that I can't seem to let out any other way, so it's very personal.

It's still afternoon, but the sun is moving toward the horizon already, the days being short at this time of year. The wind has calmed, but the wooden staircase leading down to the beach is a little on the rickety side, and it creaks and groans loudly as I make my way down. I imagine we'll be tasked with making these stairs more sturdy. When I reach the bottom, I turn and start walking northward on the beach until I find a driftwood log that looks comfortable enough, so I settle myself on it and open my sketchpad.

As usual, I get lost in my drawing, so I don't know how long I've been there when I look up to find Sam standing in front of me, a blanket under one arm and a thermos in the other hand.

"Hey there," he says, his big chocolate-colored eyes crinkling up at the corners. I don't normally think of other men as beautiful, but Sam Campbell really is. Especially with the sun shining from behind him, creating almost a halo effect around him.

"Oh, hi!" I say, appreciating how even seeing him standing in front of me causes a pleasant, warm feeling to spread throughout my belly.

"I thought it might be getting chilly down here, so a blanket and something warm to drink might be in order," he says and makes a motion for me to lift my arms so he can cover my legs with the cozy blanket. Once he's done tucking it around my legs, he grabs the thermos, unscrews the top, and pours me a travel mug of hot chocolate. Before handing it to me, he pulls something out of his pocket, and when he turns back and holds out the little cup, he's sprinkled the perfect number of mini marshmallows on top.

It's only after wrapping my hands around the warm cup that I realize how freezing I've gotten while I've been sitting here, lost in my art.

"This is so nice. Thank you so much, Sam," I say. *God, this man is going to kill me. How am I supposed to resist someone like this?*

He gives me a shy smile. "You're welcome," he says, taking a sip from his own little cup. "I thought it felt like a hot-chocolatey kind of afternoon, and you've been down here a while. I wanted to make sure you hadn't drowned or something." He chuckles, and I bump my shoulder into his, rolling my eyes.

"Haven't drowned yet. Thanks though," I reply. "This is really sweet." I take another sip, and then without thinking about it, I add, "I don't think anyone's ever brought me hot chocolate before."

I can see the sadness flash across his face, but he just nods and takes another sip of his drink. Part of the thing about being raised in a shitty family is that I don't have the same types of fond memories as people with more normal childhoods. If I'm brutally honest, my mother never showed much love to either Aaron or me when we were small. She did the bare minimum required to keep us alive. It makes it hard to connect with people who had normal parents. It sometimes feels like trying to relate to someone who's been raised by a different species. I don't know all the details about Sam's childhood, but from what I can tell, his family seems pretty normal. I've met his parents, as well as Mason and Dylan's, and they're all great. The differences between my life and Sam's are stark. We come from different worlds, with very few common experiences. Throw in the fact that I have this significant hearing loss, and it's just one more difference between us. I don't know how to be in a relationship with someone like Sam. I don't know how to be in a relationship with anyone, really. The scars I carry from my childhood and now from the Army, both mental and physical, broke me down so much I'd never be able to offer anything to someone like that. The long and the short of it is that there's no way Sam and I could ever work, no matter how much my heart might long for someone like him. Fuck, I can't even keep a decent relationship with my only sibling; I'd never be able to figure out a romantic relationship. Every relationship I've ever touched has turned to shit, and I wouldn't have a damn clue how to fit into a family dynamic that's actually healthy.

I shake my head and let out a huff of disgust, which I disguise by quickly taking a sip of my hot chocolate, doing my best to shove those thoughts aside. Sam is a nice guy, and maybe we'll get to know each other over the next few months. Hopefully, we can be friends. That's the best I can hope for, and I'll take what I can get.

CHAPTER 14

SAM

Sitting beside Tyler on the driftwood log, drinking hot chocolate and staring out to the ocean, feels like the perfect way to wind down the day. After he left for the beach, I puttered around, fixing the gas fireplace in the guest cabin and getting things settled for us, but when he'd been gone a while, I started to get concerned. Again with the weird, protective instinct toward Tyler. I still can't figure it out. I saw the sketchbook he had tucked under his arm, so I figured he must have gotten distracted. He's mentioned once or twice that he draws as part of his therapy, which I've always thought was cool, but I've never seen any of his artwork. Maybe he'll let me while we're roommates.

Once the sun started to set, I knew the temperature would drop quickly, so I decided to check on him. I didn't really want him to know that's what I was doing, which is how I ended up bringing him hot chocolate, but I'm glad I did. It's the perfect way to end the afternoon.

I still have no idea what we're going to do about the sleeping arrangements. For a few nights, one of us sleeping on the couch wouldn't be a big deal, but since we're going to be here for several months, I'm going to have to talk to Mason and figure something else out.

We sit silently for a bit, but once the sun drops into the ocean, the temperature goes from chilly to friggin' freezing. I turn to Tyler to find him clutching his now cold cup of hot chocolate and shivering.

"Shit, Tyler, you're freezing," I say, hopping up and taking the cup from his hand. I grab the blanket from around his legs and wrap it around his shoulders. After I gather up the thermos and put everything back in my backpack, I wrap one arm around him, pulling him close to me and hoping that will help him stop shivering.

"Come on, Freezy Bear. It's too cold to be sitting out here. Let's go back to the cabin. I got the fireplace working, and I'll get the steaks going for dinner."

Tyler nods in response, his teeth chattering from the cold. "I didn't actually realize how cold it had gotten," he murmurs, pulling the blanket more tightly around his shoulders as we make our way to the staircase.

"Your brain was busy with other stuff." I'd caught just a glimpse of the sketch he was working on when I'd first approached. It looked like one of the hunched-over, windblown trees perched on the edge of the cliff, and it looked beautiful. I would love to see the rest of his work, but as soon as I sat down beside him, he snapped his book closed abruptly, and I didn't want to pry.

The more I get to know him, the more I feel like I don't know. Tyler is a closed book, but I want to learn more about him. I want to open the book and see what's on every page of him. I get the feeling he carries a heavy load, one he doesn't share with anyone else. I don't understand my desire to help him carry his burden though. In all my many, *many* relationships, I don't recall this need to take on someone else's baggage. It's like some kind of compulsion. I don't want to push him, but I hope as we get to know each other, he'll let me in and allow me to help. I have no idea what keeps him so weighed down all the time, but I know I'd do nearly anything to lighten his load.

We approach the bottom of the staircase just as the last sliver of orange sun disappears behind the horizon, and I'm glad we headed back when we did since it's almost totally dark already.

Ten minutes later, we're back in the guesthouse. It really is a perfect little love nest. If only we were in love. A wistful sigh escapes me at the thought, but thankfully, Tyler doesn't notice.

Even after our scorching-hot encounter a couple of weeks ago, I'm not naive enough to think that there could truly be anything between us. For one thing, I'm way older than he is, so much older that I'm on the alarmingly close to "creepy old man" territory. He's so young, how would we ever find common ground? Not to mention the fact that we work together, and I really don't want to be *that* guy. Not that I'm technically Tyler's boss, but still.

Pulling my attention back into the present, I find Tyler staring at me with a confused look. "Sorry, man, I spaced out for a second. What'd you say?" I ask, shaking my head, trying to get rid of the cobwebs.

He grins at me, his face lighting up. He usually wears a tense expression and pastes on a smile when he knows someone's watching him. But when he gifts you with a genuine smile... wow, is it ever worth it.

"I was just wondering what I can do to help with dinner?" he asks, his lips curling up at the corners, like he's trying not to chuckle at me spacing out. I had grabbed a couple of delicious-looking steaks at the little grocery store and promised to grill them up for us on the BBQ we had found in the small shed adjacent to the cabin. This place isn't going to be difficult to spend a couple of months in—it's nicer than my condo, for god's sake.

"Um. Yeah, right. I'll go fire up the grill. Why don't you throw together the salad?" I say, heading to the door.

A little while later, I step back into the kitchen carrying a plate of delicious steaks grilled to perfection. Yeah, we bought way too much, but there will be leftovers for this week when we'll be too tired from work to think about cooking. Tyler has everything else ready, and he's puttering around the kitchen. The whole scene is strangely domestic, and I like it, but I can't let myself like it too much. That's how I end up falling head over heels with people who aren't right for me.

"Are you a wine drinker?" I ask, and his cheeks turn a sweet shade of pink that makes my tummy do a little flip. I really need to stop imagining what he would look like with that adorable flush spreading over the rest of his body. My cock twitches in my jeans, and I give myself a stern, silent talking-to. My dick needs to get the memo that this cannot happen. Again. This cannot happen again.

"Um, no. I'm not really a wine drinker. But I'll have a glass," he says, peering up at me through his lashes, and Jesus fuck, my knees nearly give out. That look makes me want to tear his clothes off and push him up against the countertop, kissing and grinding against him until we're both breathless.

"I'm no expert, but I know I like this one, so let's go for it," I say, uncorking the bottle and quickly pouring us each a glass. Fuck the whole "let it breathe" concept. I need something to mellow me out right now. I don't want to let myself enjoy how comfortable this whole thing is. Making dinner together and being domestic and cozy is everything I've ever truly wanted. Spending an evening like this fits me perfectly, like a good pair of jeans. I have the weird feeling of being exactly where I'm meant to be, although I know that's just my poor heart longing for something it can't have.

CHAPTER 15

TYLER

Sam and I working together to make dinner is kind of surreal. I don't want to admit how good it feels to have someone go to the trouble of making a nice dinner to share with me. Strangely, none of my bar bathroom hookups have wanted that.

When he comes in from the BBQ, the smell of grilled meat makes my mouth water. He sets the platter down on the counter with a flourish and waves the tongs around like a magic wand. "Your dinner, kind sir," he says, and he's such a goof I can't help but laugh. He's too damn sweet not to.

A few minutes later, we're sitting at the table, our delicious meals in front of us. Sam tops up our wine and sends me a fond look.

"Well, this is it. The beginning of our adventure on the wild and woolly Washington coast. Hope you're up for it," he says. We both laugh before taking a drink, and then it's quiet for a few moments while we dig in. I don't know if it's all the fresh ocean air I got this afternoon, the long drive, or just a function of being here, but it's one of the best meals I've ever had. I'm so wrapped up in the food I'm almost startled when Sam speaks.

"I texted Mason while the steaks were on the grill," he says. "He messaged the owner and expects to hear back tomorrow. Whatever the owner says though, we'll figure out the sleeping situation. I don't want you to worry about it." Concern is etched across his face, and I hate that I've put it there. I don't want him to worry about me. In fact, I don't want Sam to worry about anything.

In the pit of my stomach, a little stab of disappointment pokes me. I shouldn't be surprised. Sam's a professional, and I know he wants me to feel comfortable here. There's no way he's going to make a move on me. In the back of my mind, I think I was hoping the "only one bed" situation might lead to something more... but that's clearly not going to happen.

I force a smile. "We'll figure it out. I really am fine with taking turns on the couch, you know."

"Nope. No way, dude. You came back from the Middle East missing one of your five senses and chunks of Taliban IED embedded in your body as a souvenir. There is absolutely no fucking way I'm letting you sleep on the couch. We'll figure something else out."

I roll my eyes, but I can tell arguing won't get me far. Evidently, Sam can be very determined when he wants to be. My dick appears to think this stubborn streak is meant to be sexy as it twitches under the table.

"Speaking of your service," he says between bites. "What made you decide to join up? Was the military something you always wanted to do?"

I never know how much is socially acceptable to share when I get asked this question. The only reason I joined the military was to get the hell away from my life. Things were already heading down a path that wasn't leading anywhere good, and I had to get out.

"No, I hadn't really thought about joining up until I was pretty close to graduation, actually," I say, and Sam nods.

"So what made you want to do it?"

"I wanted out of Tacoma, and there was no other way open to me." I shrug, taking another bite of steak before continuing. "As you might have guessed from this afternoon, my childhood was kind of a shitshow." I snort, giving my head a shake. "I never knew my father, and my mom wasn't exactly a stable, upstanding citizen. She was an alcoholic with a bad co-dependency habit. She'd get hooked up with a guy and would follow him to the ends of the earth, doing anything he asked, including ignoring and effectively abandoning her two kids."

Sam sets down his silverware and reaches across the table, putting his hand on mine. "Hey, you don't have to talk about this if you don't want to. I didn't mean to pry, I'm sorry." His eyes are filled with concern.

"No, it's fine. It's not a secret or anything," I say. "Anyway, my senior year of high school, Mom wasn't around. She'd followed her latest man, yet again, to some shithole town. I don't even remember where. My older brother, Aaron, had been planning to move to Nashville, but he ended up staying with me so I could graduate. I'd wanted to be an art teacher, but my grades were nowhere near good enough to get me into college, and even if they were, I'd never have been able to afford it."

I stare at the table, running my thumb along the edge of the wood. When I look up, I brace myself, expecting to see pity on Sam's face. But while he looks concerned, he also looks interested. Most people, especially if they're from nice, middle-class backgrounds, are uncomfortable with "tales of the poor in America" like the one from my childhood. Often, they act like I'm some kind of charity case or, worse, some kind of leper, like if they get too close to me, the stink of my poverty-stricken childhood will somehow rub off on them, so they want to get as far away from the subject as possible.

Sam shakes his head. "Fuck. That's rough for a kid. I'm sorry you had to deal with that shit."

I shrug again. "It is what it is. But anyway, my high school art teacher kind of took me under his wing. He would have me over for dinner a few nights a week with his family. He had a couple of daughters who were in college, but I think he'd always wanted a son, so he kind of took a shine to me." I laugh, thinking about Mr. Davison and his wife, Elaine.

"Anyway, he put the idea in my head about joining up so that when I came back, I could use the GI bill to go to college to become an art teacher, like I wanted. I wasn't super stoked about it, but I really wanted to go to college, and the military seemed like the most straightforward way to make it happen."

I lean back, taking a sip of wine, as Sam gives me a confused look.

"But if you wanted to go to college, why aren't you doing that now?" he asks. "How come you're working with us?"

"I have a few more years to use it. When I got home, I wasn't in the right headspace." I snort. "That's a very diplomatic way of putting it. The truth is, I was a hot fucking mess. I was getting blackout drunk every night because I couldn't deal with what had happened to me, and to top it off, my mother's dementia had gotten so bad that she had to go into a care home. My brother dealt with that, but it was just another thing, you know?" I take a drink of wine, not meeting Sam's eyes. I hate talking about my family, especially my mother, but there's something about the way Sam listens that makes it a little easier.

"I didn't realize your mom was in a care home. Fuck, man, you're carrying a lot on your shoulders." Sam shakes his head. But there's no pity on his face, and for the first time ever, I don't feel shame as I'm talking about my life. Sam accepts it, accepts me, without judging.

"So, is your mom in Tacoma?" he asks.

I nod. "Yeah. Most of the time, she doesn't remember who I am, and I think my visits make her agitated, so I don't go much."

"That really sucks," Sam says, shaking his head. "Are you close with your brother?"

Ah, there's the hard question. I suppose I could gloss over the shitshow my relationship with Aaron has become, but Sam is so genuine, like he actually wants to know, that I feel safe telling him. I clear my throat.

"When we were little, Aaron and I were super close. He was my best friend and my protector. He made sure I went to school, had clothes that fit, and he would even bring home art supplies for me sometimes." I let out a little chuckle, remembering. "When I was really little, they would just be crayons or markers he would swipe from his own classroom, but when he got older, he'd sometimes buy me things at the art store with money from his part-time job. Nothing fancy, but I always had a set of colored pencils and some blank paper so I could draw or sketch when I felt like it." I pause to take a sip of wine, and Sam just gives me an encouraging smile.

"I was always into drawing and coloring and stuff, but Aaron always loved music; he's super talented. He held off on his dream of moving to Nashville after high school so he could be there for me until I graduated, because he knew my mom wasn't going to step up. He waited until after I joined the Army to move. It was a huge sacrifice on his part." I swallow, knowing this is the part that might change the way Sam sees me.

"Anyway, things with our mother went downhill at lightning speed, and just as he was beginning to make a name for himself down there, he had to come back to Tacoma to deal with her. I was gone, so he was alone, trying to figure out what was wrong with her. At first, he thought it was just that she was drinking more than usual, but eventually, she got the diagnosis of Alzheimer's."

"Oh, Tyler, I'm sorry," Sam says, his eyes shining with sincerity.

"Yeah, well, don't feel too sorry for me. I didn't have to cope with her. And then when I did come home, I was still kind of fucked-up from the injury and stuff, and I didn't do anything to help him."

"But I'm sure he understands why," Sam says. "I mean, you had a life-changing injury, plus PTSD. You weren't exactly in a place to help."

I shrug, not wanting to get into the gritty details of the horrible fight Aaron and I had a couple of years ago that still haunts me.

"Yeah, I had stuff going on, but it's still not an excuse," I say. But I don't want to continue this line of conversation. "Anyway, once I started working with Derek as my therapist, things started turning around. He encouraged me to apply at HDH, and the rest is history,"

Sam smiles and takes my hint, not asking any more questions about Aaron.

"Oh, right, I forgot you came to us through Derek." He smiles fondly. "He's a great dude. Gracie May picked herself a good one."

"Yeah, Derek pretty much saved me. I was totally lost when I first came home. And I was heading down a pretty dark path, making a lot of dumb choices. Derek helped me get back on my feet."

Sam's smile is full of pride, but there's something lurking behind it. Before I can figure out what it is, he gets up from the table and busies himself with tidying up, the strange expression replaced by a cheeky grin. "Well, I'll say this, Tyler Ritchie. However, it was you ended up here, Hot Dam Homes is damn lucky to have you."

CHAPTER 16

SAM

"More wine?" I ask Tyler as I clear our dishes. I'm glad he's happy working at Hot Dam Homes; it really is a great company. Mason and Dylan are building something special, and I'm proud to be part of it. I just don't know if it's a place I'm going to be able to stay, even though that's always been my plan. But since Mason bought in as a full partner, things have been weird. The last thing I would ever want to do is put my relationship with Mason in danger. He's not only my cousin, he's my best friend, and I'd much rather find a new job than stay and damage our relationship. But the thought of leaving Hot Dam Homes, and even more, the thought of leaving Seattle, makes me slightly sick to my stomach. But I'm going to have to decide on the California job soon.

I top off both of our wineglasses, finishing off the bottle as Tyler and I clean up together. The silence between us is comfortable as we finish the dishes and make our way over to the couch. He Tyler sits at one end, and I take up residence at the other. Cable and internet access won't be set up for a few days, and the cell service is too spotty to watch anything on our phones, so we sit, nursing the last of our wine, and keep talking. It's strangely nice to sit with someone and have that "getting to know each other" conversation without the pressure of it being a first date. Since my last relationship ended, I've held off on dating. I've spent the last year or so trying to figure out what I actually want from my life. And now, with the weird tension between Mason and me, I keep wondering if the universe is trying to tell me it's time to make a real change. Maybe that job in California is what I need to do. Fuck if I know.

We talk about everything and nothing for a long time, and I'm struck by how different our lives have been. Even though I'm an only child, I grew up surrounded by family, and though it was far from perfect, one thing I've never doubted is how much they love me. I've always wanted to have a big family of my own, partly because of the way I grew up. I would have loved a sibling, but my parents weren't able to have more kids, so I ended up with the next best thing. On the other hand, Tyler's next best thing was getting blown up in the Afghan desert. Even though he's only in his twenties, Tyler has dealt with a lot more in his life than I have, at nearly forty.

The evening seems to fly past, and when we both yawn, I glance at my phone to see it's well after midnight.

"Shit, I didn't realize how late it was. I'm ready to hit the sack. How about you?" I ask, and Tyler nods, unsuccessfully covering up another yawn as he does so.

"Don't even try to argue that you're taking the couch. It's not happening," I say with a mock threatening look. "I told Mason about the single giant-ass bed in here, and after he stopped laughing, he told us to get one of those fancy air beds. It will be easy to take it down during the day if we need to and put it up when I go to bed."

Tyler hesitates for a second, like he might be thinking about arguing, but instead, he shrugs.

A move I shouldn't find endearing but totally do.

"Okay, well, if you're that insistent about it, I won't argue about taking the huge bed all to myself, sprawling out everywhere and rolling around in all that space."

Our eyes meet unexpectedly, and there's a weird moment of awkwardness while I imagine Tyler rolling around in the sheets. Only in my imagination, I'm right there with him, helping to make very good use of all the space in the huge bed.

He clears his throat. "What about tonight though?"

"For tonight, I am perfectly happy to make myself comfy on the couch," I say firmly, getting up to grab the extra sheets and blankets I spied in a closet earlier. Tyler laughs and goes into the bathroom to get ready for bed.

A few minutes later, I'm finishing making up my couch-bed when I look up to see him coming out of bathroom looking delicious, all scrubbed clean and comfy-looking. He's wearing loose plaid sleep pants, and I'm pretty sure he's going commando under them. I can't make out the design of the tattoos peeking out from under his short sleeves, but the bright colors are visible through his thin white T-shirt spreading across his chest. His shoulders are narrower than mine, but I know the hidden strength they hold. His body is the perfect balance of power and grace as he walks toward me, and my cock hardens so fast I feel like it's about to bust out of my jeans with a "boi-oi-oi-oi-oing" sound.

"Hey, dude," I choke out, desperately hoping he doesn't have his hearing aids in so maybe he won't hear the way my voice cracks.

"Hey," he says. I swear his gaze lingers on my crotch a second too long, but he shakes his head, and the moment is gone as quickly as it appeared.

"Okay, well, I'm going to hit the hay, I guess," he says, directing a shy smile at me.

"I'm right behind you. Going to get cleaned up, and I'll probably be passed out in five minutes. If I snore, feel free to drop a pillow down on me or something," I say, not really thinking about who I'm talking to. I start to stutter in embarrassment, but Tyler just chuckles.

"Lucky for you, I don't sleep with my hearing aids in, so you can snore as loud as you want."

"Man, I bet my last girlfriend wished she had the ability to turn her hearing off. She hated my snoring."

"I guess it has its perks, at times." He smiles softly and turns to head up to the loft.

"Good night, Tyler," I say, and before I can stop myself, I reach for him, as if to give him a hug. I try to cover it up by making it seem like I'm walking into the kitchen instead of toward him, but I don't think he buys it. There's a strange energy between us as he turns to climb up to his bedroom. He rustles around for a few minutes before settling on that giant bed. I swallow, trying to think about anything other than how he might look all tangled up in the sheets, sweaty and flushed after I've fucked him until he screams.

I really need to rein in this crush on Tyler. It's not going to make working and living together very comfortable if I'm constantly popping wood every time he's around. *Fucking hell.*

As I suspected, the damn couch is not comfortable, so it takes me a while to fall asleep, and when I do, I'm tortured with dreams of a gorgeous Army veteran with tattoos I'm dying to trace with my tongue.

CHAPTER 17

TYLER

The first two weeks on the coast fly by so fast I'm not convinced we didn't somehow end up in a crazy time warp. It turns out that when I don't have to bookend my workday sitting in never-ending traffic, I actually really fucking love this job. And working with Sam is amazing. We've fallen into a routine, and every day, we get a little more comfortable with each other. The awkwardness of the first night we spent at the cabin passed quickly, both of us motivated to make the situation work. The routine of Sam sleeping in the fancy air bed and me in the loft upstairs has become comfortable, and I like falling asleep knowing he's just downstairs from me.

Friday afternoon of our second full week out at Ocean Shores, the sun is shining brightly through the windows of the main lodge while Sam enjoys himself swinging the sledgehammer into a wall we're removing. It's my turn to take the debris out to the big dumpster. Under the owner's instructions, we're keeping everything we think we can repurpose, but unfortunately, there's still a lot of stuff that needs to go to the landfill. Using the sledgehammer is surprisingly therapeutic, so we're taking turns with it. I spent about a half hour imagining I was beating the crap out of the Taliban fighter who set the IED that took my hearing. It was almost as good as a therapy session with Derek.

"Hey, Ty, how about doing something fun tonight?" Sam asks toward the end of the day.

"Um, sure. What are you thinking?"

"Bonfire down on the beach! It's so calm today we shouldn't waste the opportunity."

I think for a moment and then wonder why I'm hesitating. It's not like I have other plans, and a beach bonfire sounds pretty fucking cool.

"Yeah, that sounds awesome. What do we need for that?" I ask.

"I'll do a grocery run as soon as we're done here. We'll want to get things set up before the sun goes down. I'll grab some hot dogs and buns and the makings for s'mores."

I smile. Sam's enthusiasm for all things is infectious. I love the way he's so naturally positive and optimistic. It's so different from me—I'm always waiting for the other shoe to drop, even when things are going great.

We get things cleaned up quickly, and Sam heads to the store while I take a few trips down the beach stairs, ferrying firewood and other supplies. Might as well make myself useful.

A while later, I've got things set up, or at least I think they're set up. It's not like I have any experience with beach bonfires or making s'mores, but it can't be that complicated. The sun is starting to head toward the horizon, but it's still providing enough warmth that I can feel the promise of spring in the air. I hold my face up to it, reveling in the warmth on my skin, when suddenly, I'm overcome with a memory of my mom so strong I have to swallow back tears.

There was a period of time when I was maybe five or six, and Mom must have been doing well since she was there a lot—more than usual. I don't remember a guy being around, so maybe she was going through a rare period of standing on her own two feet. I recall one afternoon in our shitty apartment, me and Aaron and Mom. She was playing music, which in itself was strange because normally the TV was always blaring in the background. Aaron was lying on the couch, reading a magazine or something. He must have been twelve or thirteen. I was sitting on the floor playing with trucks, and this song came on. "These Are Days" by 10,000 Maniacs. My mom turned up the volume and started to sing, and I just remember both Aaron and me looking at her with our mouths hanging open. It was so unlike her. Her voice was so pure as she sang along with Natalie Merchant. She came over to us from where she'd been standing in the kitchen and grabbed both our hands, and the three of us held hands and danced around our living room. The lyrics are fuzzy in my memory, like they've been locked away in some lost, hidden corner of my mind for so long they're literally covered in dust, but their meaning is seared into my brain.

She sang about being blessed and lucky, about days filled with laughter, and how when you feel the sunlight warm your face, those are the days you'd know how life was meant to be.

I can almost feel their hands in mine, and I can hear the music in my head as plain as day. I close my eyes and let the sun warm my face, like the song says. I let myself get carried away by the memory of my mom as a happy, strong person and of the three of us being together and feeling like an actual family instead of screaming and fighting with each other.

That's how Sam finds me a few minutes later, sitting on a driftwood log, letting the sun make its way across my face. When a shadow drifts over me, I open my eyes to find him looking at me with an expression that nearly burns me with its intensity. I've never seen anyone look at me with so much raw hunger. Reaching out, he cups the side of my face with his hand, stunning me for a second.

"I really want to kiss you right now," he breathes softly. I can't hear him over the sound of the ocean, but I feel his voice and see his lips move. Heat spreads through my belly.

"Yeah?" I ask breathlessly. "Then you should do it."

He doesn't wait for another invitation, leaning down to place the softest whisper of a kiss on my lips. Pulling back, he searches my eyes before standing and pulling me up with him and kissing me again. This kiss is harder and deeper but not rough. His lips are soft and full, and I feel rather than hear his groan as he pulls me into him. I don't resist, allowing my body to melt against his. Electricity surges through me, and I'm buzzing with need as I press myself even closer, molding myself to his shape, wanting no space between us.

Finally, we break apart, needing oxygen. Sam rests his forehead against mine as we both catch our breaths.

"Hi," he whispers, his breath warm on my cheek.

"Um, yeah. Hi."

We both chuckle, and I'm finding it impossible to remember why I've been so desperately trying to resist my attraction to him. Our slightly awkward but still hot-as-fuck hookup a few weeks earlier was nothing but an appetizer if this kiss is anything to go on. My heart is still pounding as he presses his lips softly to my forehead and steps back, turning around and immediately getting to work on building a fire as I plant myself on the sand to watch him.

A few minutes later, we're sitting in front of a lovely roaring fire. It radiates a comforting glow as the flames reach for the soft purple-gray sky above us. Warmth wraps around me like a cozy blanket, making me notice the cool, firm sand I'm sitting on.

"This is awesome," I say as he repositions one of the logs "to make sure we get the best kind of coals for roasting," whatever that means.

"Thanks," he says, a proud little grin playing on his lips. "It was usually my dad or sometimes my uncle Bob, Mason's dad, who was in charge of fire duties, so I feel like I've just gone through a sacred rite of passage," he chortles. "Now we just need to wait a little, then we can start roasting the dogs."

He rummages around in his big backpack for a minute and pulls out a couple of warm-looking blankets. He spreads one on the ground to keep our butts off the cold sand, and when I scooch onto it, he drapes the second one over my legs. Between the heat from the fire, the lingering warmth of the setting sun, and my fond memory of my childhood, I'm feeling as content as I ever do.

The next thing to come out of Sam's magical backpack is a six-pack of beer, and he hands me one. It's only the second time we've had alcohol since we've been here. Neither one of us are big drinkers, it turns out. I don't know if it's the atmosphere and all the fresh air or the good feelings I have floating around inside my chest right now, but the beer feels fantastic going down, and I grab another as soon as the first one is gone.

The conversation between us flows easily as we watch the fire. I feel like there's nothing I couldn't say to Sam, and I wish I'd allowed myself to get to know him sooner.

"Do you think you'll stay around Hot Dam Homes for a long time?" I ask him out of the blue. I don't really know where the question came from, but I'm curious about him. I want to know his dreams and his goals and what drives him. I want to know what makes him happy and what hurts him and his biggest fears. I've never found myself ever wanting to really know those things about another person, but Sam is different in a lot of ways.

He gives me a thoughtful look. "I assumed I'd stay for a long time," he says, letting out a breath and looking down at his beer bottle. "But... Can you keep a secret?" he asks.

"Sure, of course," I say.

He sighs. "Things have been different for a while now. I don't know if it's because Mason's gone full partner with Dylan or some other reason, or maybe it's just me and it's all in my head. But it doesn't feel the same as it used to." He pauses to take a swig of his beer and continues.

"I have an opportunity to move down to Southern California. No one knows about it. A friend from school started a company down there, and he wants me to buy in and help him run it." Sam pauses and takes another drink before sighing heavily. "I never, ever thought I'd leave the PNW, but I don't know. I feel like it might be time for me to shake up my life in some way."

A stab of uncertainty slices through my gut at his words. He's thinking about leaving? Not only leaving Hot Dam Homes but leaving Seattle altogether? I know how close their family is, and I can only imagine how devastated everyone will be if he leaves.

He must sense my unease, and he waves a hand dismissively. "It's nothing for you to be worried about though. I told Shane that if I say yes, I'll stay here to finish this job. It's just that... I don't know the right thing to do. I'm pretty sure it's my own crap making me feel weird, and I don't know if taking another job and moving will make things better or if it's just running away, you know?"

"What do you mean by 'your own crap'?" I ask.

Sam blows out a heavy breath before draining the last of his beer and reaching for another. "It's nothing Mason or Dylan or anyone else is doing. I think I've been trying to avoid admitting to myself that the stuff that's bothering me is coming from inside, not outside."

I give him a questioning look, and he shrugs uncomfortably.

"I'm kind of insecure, and when I saw Mason stepping up and growing in his career, I felt... inadequate. Like I'm not enough. I'm ordinary and boring, and I'll never be a real success at anything. But all those are my hang-ups, based on my long list of failed relationships and my never-ending search for 'the one' that never works out." He pauses, nervously peeling the label off his beer bottle. "None of this is based on anything Mason or Dylan did or said. It's not even really coming from anything work related. I just feel like I'm not good enough sometimes... not for a relationship that lasts, not for a career, not for anything important to me. I don't know if moving away will make things better or worse for my insecure little pea-brain." He shakes his head and turns to rummage around in the cooler. "But you don't want to hear about my messed-up midlife-crisis bullshit. Let's roast some dogs."

CHAPTER 18

SAM

Smooth change of subject, Sam. I roll my eyes internally as I busy myself getting Tyler set up with a hot dog on a stick. Once I've shown him the best way to hold his wiener so it cooks perfectly—and yes, all puns are welcome—I get my own organized, angling myself so I can lean back against the log as I hold my arm out over the fire.

"My ex-girlfriend really messed with my head," I blurt out, and Tyler jerks his head up as I jump right back into the conversation I cut off abruptly a few minutes ago. He cocks an eyebrow at me.

"Jessica?" he asks, and I nod. "I only met her a few times when she visited you at work, but she always seemed nice."

"She was—is—nice. She wasn't trying to hurt me when we broke up. She was just... brutally honest, I guess."

"What do you mean?"

I blow out a breath, pushing the air out of my lungs while I stare into the fire.

"We were together for over a year. I really liked her. I thought I loved her, but I'm not as sure about that anymore. Anyway, we got to that place in the relationship where we either needed to take the next step or break up. I wanted to take the next step, and she wanted to break up."

"I'm sorry, Sam. That probably felt like shit."

"Yeah, it really did. This is a little humiliating, but I'd even made plans to go ring shopping. Mason was going to come with me." I shake my head ruefully. "She beat me to the punch, though, and dumped me before I could ask her. Which I guess is a good thing."

Tyler's eyes widen, and he gives me a sympathetic smile. "Shit. But yeah, I guess that would have been worse."

I sigh. "She told me I wasn't finding the right person because I was trying too hard to be someone I'm not. She said she couldn't love me because I wasn't okay with myself. That deep down, I'm not happy with who I am, and it's a major turnoff."

"Oh, whoa. That seems kind of... harsh," Tyler says.

"The thing is, she was totally right." I breathe out a heavy sigh. "I've always had this... inferiority complex, I guess. And there's no good reason for it. My parents are amazing, and even though I'm an only child, I was folded into Mason's family, and my cousins became my siblings, so I was never the 'lonely only child.' But I've always had this hang-up that I'm not enough, like there's nothing interesting or remarkable about me. Honest to fuck, if you looked up the word 'average' in the dictionary, my photo's there. I was an average student, I drive an average car, I make an average salary, yada yada yada. Anyway, it's not a big jump to get from Average Guy to 'as exciting as watching paint dry,' so I've always tried to be whatever my boyfriend or girlfriend wanted, or at least what I thought they wanted."

Why the hell I'm spilling all these deep, dark thoughts all over Tyler, I have no idea. I've never talked about this stuff with anyone, not even Mason.

"Oh, Sam," Tyler says quietly.

"I thought about it a lot, and I think she was right though. So, I haven't dated anyone since we broke up. I've been trying to figure out how to 'be myself,' whatever the fuck that means." I laugh bitterly. Fuck, talk about trying to scare a guy off. Spilling this shit makes me sound like a pathetic, sad sack. I have no idea why, but I feel safe telling Tyler, even though I'm embarrassed as hell right now.

He shifts so he's staring straight into my eyes. "Sam, I hope you know none of that is true. You can't compare yourself to anyone else. You, Sam, you're... incredible... Wonderful... Amazing..."

I force a smile, but I know it isn't reaching my eyes. "That's sweet of you to say, but I mean, you've met my cousins. They're all these exceptional people. Mason has this incredible presence, this aura around him that everyone's drawn to. And Gracie's smart as hell, with this firecracker of a personality. And Dylan is, like, this super-impressive guy. Not everyone gets him right away because they misunderstand his autism. But he makes such a strong impression on everyone because he's this incredible person who's totally different than anyone else." I let out a snort.

"And then there's good ol' cousin Sammy. I am the most average guy you could possibly imagine," I laugh, but when he starts to protest, I wave at Tyler to stop him. "I'm serious. It's just the facts."

I'm talking fast, and I can only hope he's getting most of it. Embarrassing as it is, I feel like I need to get these thoughts out, otherwise I just might fucking explode.

I'm breathless as I finish talking. My cheeks are burning hot with shame, and I keep my eyes off him as I look around for something to keep my hands occupied. We forgot about our hot dogs during my embarrassing word vomit, both still holding them mindlessly over the flames, but somehow, they still look edible. I grab a couple of buns out of the bag, handing one over without raising my eyes to look at him, and then I concentrate really hard on getting my hot dog perfectly aligned in the bun and adding ketchup and mustard like I'm painting a masterpiece. Tyler still hasn't said a word.

We eat our hot dogs in silence, and the awkwardness presses down on me so hard I feel like my chest is about to burst open. *Fuckity fuck, is he going to say anything?* I've probably made him so uncomfortable he's dying to get the fuck away from me.

I'm so preoccupied with being embarrassed I don't notice him shift to his knees and shuffle toward me until he swings one leg over mine, straddling my legs, which are stretched out in front of me.

I look up, meeting his eyes as he reaches for me, cradling my face gently in both hands and holding me so I can't look away. His hands are cold on my skin, but his touch heats me up from the deepest part of my gut. He stares into my eyes, and I swallow nervously. Then he leans down and presses his mouth to mine. At first, I freeze, but very quickly, my body responds.

I lean into the kiss, responding eagerly, and he shuffles even closer so our dicks press together through our jeans as he kisses me like there's no tomorrow. I wrap my arms around him, and he threads his hands into my slightly too-long hair, his fingers cold against my scalp.

I don't know how long we kiss. It could be a minute, ten minutes, or an hour. All my blood rushed south to my cock as soon as he started kissing me, and I'm as hard as I've ever been. We grind against each other, feeding each other soft moans.

Breaking apart, I press my forehead against his, closing my eyes for a moment.

"Wow," I say. "Maybe I should spill all my darkest secrets more often if this is how you react."

He gives me a gentle smile, but his eyes are serious. "I can feel how insecure you are about this stuff. But please, please hear me, Sam. Average doesn't mean being boring. You are one of the best people I've ever met. You're reliable, and kind, and thoughtful. The fact that you're not six foot six like Mason, or that you didn't graduate at the top of your class like Grace, or whatever else you're feeling inferior over... none of that means shit. You're sincere and funny, and you have one of the best hearts of anyone I've ever known. Being dependable and reliable doesn't make you boring; it makes you a solid person. Someone people know they can count on. You're using those amazing qualities to tear yourself down when those qualities are some of the best things about you. I think you're a fucking incredible person."

There's a pause while I swallow the lump in my throat. No one has ever said anything so simple but so meaningful to me.

"Thank you," I whisper.

"Don't thank me. It's the truth." He kisses me gently, brushing my cheek with his fingertips.

He pulls back a moment later, and we search each other's eyes, for what, I don't know. A moment later, his mouth curves into a mischievous grin. "So, I believe I was promised lessons in s'more making?"

"Let's do it," I reply as he shifts off my lap, and I dig out the marshmallows, chocolate, and graham crackers from the backpack. Tyler pulls me down onto the blanket beside him, and we spend the next hour snuggled together while I teach him how to make the best s'mores in the entire world.

CHAPTER 19

TYLER

I can't breathe. My mouth and nose are full of dirt, suffocating me. I cough and sputter until I can take a gasping breath. The searing heat from the fire surrounds me, so hot it feels like my clothes are melting. My eyes are stinging, and the world has turned from color to shades of brown and gray. My palms are bloody from scraping against the sharp gravel beneath me, and there's a bright red stain creeping across my abdomen. My ears are ringing so loud I feel like I'm underwater. Every inch of me burns with pain, but I force myself to move. I'm disoriented and confused, but I know I need to get away before the flames reach me. My weapon. I need my weapon. I reach for it, but my arm won't work. I look down and see why.

Everything below my elbow has been twisted around like it's on backward. I don't know what to do, and panic starts to rise in my chest. I'm going to die here in this godforsaken desert. There's a body a few feet away from me. It's Paddy, my platoon leader, and I don't know if he's alive or dead. I start to shake violently, and I just know I'm going to die here.

I snap my eyes open to find Sam leaning over me, his hands on my shoulders, shaking me awake. His mouth is moving—I think he's repeating my name over and over. I sit up suddenly and grab his arm, bile rising in my throat. "I'm gonna be sick," I choke out, and with lightning speed, Sam grabs a wastebasket and sets it in front of me just in time for me to empty my guts into it. Tears run down my face as I shake, retching uncontrollably, over and over. I can't hear anything, but I can feel Sam running his hand up and down my back, trying to soothe me. Finally, it's over, and I lean back shakily, wiping my mouth with the back of my hand. "I'm sorry. Oh my god, I'm so, so sorry," I repeat over and over as I reach for my hearing aids on the nightstand, my hands still trembling so hard it takes a couple of tries for me to get them inserted properly.

"Hey," Sam says once I get my aids working. There's no way I can look him in the eyes. I am so goddamn humiliated. It's a small consolation that I haven't pissed myself on top of puking all over the place, but somehow, that doesn't make things much better. I'm still breathing heavily as I continue to apologize, my mind spinning out of control, flipping out about how I'm never going to be able to face Sam again. How this thing I was most afraid of, Sam seeing what my nightmares do to me, has now happened, and I don't know what I'm going to do.

Sam lets me catch my breath, and then he takes my chin gently and turns my head so I have to look at him. "Do not apologize to me. Do. Not. If you keep doing it, I'm gonna be insulted. You *lived* whatever experience gives you those nightmares. You *survived*. You should never be ashamed of that. If I can help you cope with some of this shit, that's a fucking honor for me. You got that?" he says, a thread of steel running through his voice I haven't heard before. It's comforting, making me feel safe and causing heat to flare low down in my belly.

I nod, looking at him, still breathing shallow-ly. He lets go of my chin and wraps me in his arms, pulling me close to him, and we just sit there for a little while.

A few minutes later, he speaks with a gentle voice. "Will you be okay for a few minutes if I go clean up? Or I can help you downstairs. Do you think a shower might help you feel better?" he asks.

"Yeah, I'll, um. I'll go shower and brush my teeth. Um... Thanks, Sam."

I'm a little wobbly as I follow him down the ladder to the main floor, but he stays close behind me, which helps. After he ducks into the bathroom to clean up the trash can, which I try not to think about, he turns on the shower, letting the water warm up for me. After he shuts the door behind him and I'm alone with my thoughts, I allow myself a few minutes to sob quietly as the hot water cascades over me. I try to imagine the water cleansing me of all the horrible memories, but I know the nightmares will return. I'm grateful they don't happen as often now, but it doesn't make them easier to deal with. I feel a little better after I let some of it out, and then I take my time to wash myself, trying to concentrate only on the physical sensations. When I shut off the water, I see that Sam has sneaked into the bathroom and set a fresh towel and clean sweatpants and a T-shirt on the counter for me. I almost get choked up again. I don't care what he says, there's no way I'll ever be able to repay the kindness he's showing me. I'm so broken, and he doesn't even seem to notice.

I dry off and get dressed quickly, brush my teeth thoroughly, and hang the towel up neatly on the rack before exiting the bathroom. When I climb back up to the loft, he's there, just finishing making the bed. He's changed the sheets, and there's a glass of water and one of ginger ale sitting on the nightstand. I fight to swallow the lump in my throat.

He pulls back the blankets for me and waves me into bed. "Here you are, good sir," he says in a ridiculously over-the-top British accent and shooting me a grin. I climb in under the covers, and he shushes me when I try to speak. He makes me lie down and makes a big show of fluffing up my pillows and tucking the sheets in around me so I'm in a cocoon of soft, warm cotton. When he's finally done, he leans over me, one arm on either side of my waist.

"Are you okay?" he asks, concern written all over his face. He reaches out and tenderly caresses my cheek, and the sweet gesture feels oddly natural.

"I'm alright," I answer, but before I can think about what I'm doing, I've grabbed onto his arm. "Would you... Um... Would you stay? With me? For a bit?"

CHAPTER 20

SAM

My heart squeezes in my chest. "Of course. I'll stay as long as you need." I move quickly to slide into bed beside him and pull him close so he's cuddled into my chest, wrapping my arms around him. He needs comfort right now, and my desire to give him what he needs is stronger than anything else.

"Will it help to talk about it?" I ask. "It's okay if it doesn't, but I'll listen if it helps you." I'm no veteran, but I do know that throwing your shit into a closet and slamming the door shut, hoping it doesn't spill out and make a mess, isn't a great long-term coping strategy.

Tyler bites down on his lip before letting out a sigh. "Yeah. Sometimes it helps. But it sometimes makes the nightmares worse for a few days before they slow down again."

"You can share whatever you want or nothing at all. I just want you to know I'm here for you. No matter what."

The last thing I want to do is pressure him, but if I can help him, I'll do anything, and I want him to know that. My need to take care of and protect Tyler isn't like anything I've ever felt, but it feels so right and so natural. It sounds ridiculous, but it feels like caring for him is something I'm meant to do.

Some of the tension drains from his body, and I love the way his muscles soften as he allows himself to melt into me. His head is resting on my chest, so I dip my chin to place a kiss on top of it.

"So, I left for boot camp like four days after high school graduation," he starts. "I made it through that, and even though it sucked balls, I mostly felt like I fit in with the other guys, which was a new feeling." He huffs a laugh. "I found out pretty quick after boot camp I was getting deployed. It was going to be a fifteen-month deployment. I was living on base at the time, and we all partied hard before we shipped out.

I think that was the closest I had to a college experience." He laughs wryly.

"On the day we left, I was kind of glad I didn't have any family there to say goodbye to. I would have been more afraid, I think. The guys that did have family there had a way harder time." Tyler snorts. "Perks of having a shitty family: not having to take part in all the over-wrought goodbyes and tears and shit."

I tighten my arms around him, my heart breaking at the thought of Tyler as a skinny eighteen-year-old kid about to leave for a for-eign country, possibly to be killed, and no one even showed up to say goodbye.

He continues. "I remember the first guy who was KIA from my platoon. His name was Joey. We'd been there a few months, maybe five or six months or so, and we were going to meet with some locals in the nearest village. It was something we did all the time, about as routine as those things could get. But we got partway to the village, and there was a group of fucking goats or something standing in the road. Dan-ny, our driver, stopped and honked at them, trying to get them to move out of our way, but these stupid animals just stood there looking at us. So Joey says, 'I'll go move 'em,' and he opens the door of the Humvee and gets out to shoo these things off the road, and then he just drops to the ground. Shot by a fucking sniper."

I suck in a breath. Tyler's voice is flat, like he's disconnected from the words coming out of his mouth.

"I don't remember much after I saw him go down. I know the shit hit the fan. Total chaos. We got him back into the vehicle, and we were able to take out the sniper who killed him but obviously too late. I don't think it sank in at all for me until we got back to our base that night and Joey wasn't there. He was one of the few guys I'd really liked. He had this stupid sense of humor, you know?" There's a smile in Tyler's voice as he talks about his friend. "He would tell these ridiculous jokes, and most of the guys would just groan, but I always thought he was kind of funny. He was sweet, even though he was a fucking giant, even bigger than Mason. Complete badass with this dad's sense of humor. He was just an awesome dude."

"I'm sorry that happened to him. And to you." I place another kiss against his temple. I don't even know if he can hear my whisper with his hearing aids. But I need to say it anyway, and I try to show him with my touch how much he's affecting me.

"We had this, like, memorial service for him, and I wanted to cry, but I felt like there was no way I could. I mean, a couple of guys did, but I was one of the younger, smaller guys, and I just felt like I couldn't." He takes a shaky breath.

I stay quiet, and Tyler's heart races, thudding against my chest like a runaway freight train while outwardly, he seems completely calm. He's like a duck who looks completely placid as he moves across the water, while his legs move frantically beneath the surface.

"I got hurt a few months after we lost Joey. But, fuck, it feels like forever, you know?" He shakes his head. That day, I was out on patrol, and we were supposed to be searching for this well-known warlord guy. We were told he was a 'high-value target.' I think they suspected he was responsible for attacking a couple of convoys a few months earlier." He swallows. "So, we get to this house where they're supposed to be, and they're fucking gone. But we go in, and it's obvious they'd just been there and left in a big hurry, which means they probably got tipped off by a local. They can't have gone too far, so my platoon leader is all excited about maybe being able to catch this guy. He's talking to me about our plan, and as we're just getting back to the vehicles, he steps on a pressure plate. It blew him up, blew the closest Humvee apart, and I have no idea why it didn't blow me into a million pieces."

"Oh my god," I whisper softly. I hadn't realized Tyler had been so close to the explosion. He could have so easily been killed.

"You know, we were always watching, searching for signs of IEDs. Always trying to detect any slight difference in the way the sand or the dirt was lying on any road or any other little signs. Always, always on alert, on edge. But neither of us saw the signs of that one. I don't know why."

I squeeze him tightly to my chest, just as much for my own comfort as for his.

"I didn't know what happened at first. All of a sudden, everything around me goes gray and brown—the whole world is just dirt. I don't remember hitting the ground. It's like one second, I'm walking along, and the next second, I'm on my back, looking up at the sky through this dirty haze. I can't breathe, so I'm coughing and trying to get a breath, but it's like there's no more air—it's just sludge surrounding me.

Not being able to catch my breath is one of the most vivid memories. That's what most of my nightmares are. It's like I'm drowning but not in water. I'm drowning in dirt." He shudders and reaches out to grab the water glass off the bedside table. Once he takes a couple of sips, I take it and put it back for him before placing my arm around him again and stroking up and down his spine, trying to ground both of us with the physical sensation of touch.

"So, I finally get a breath, but I can't hear a fucking thing. I would say my ears were ringing, but it's more like my whole head was ringing. But all I can think about is that I have to get my weapon. I don't know where I am or who's around; I just know I need my weapon before anything else. I manage to sit up, and I reach my gun with one hand, and I move my other arm to hold it properly, but something doesn't feel right, so I look down, and my arm's all twisted up. It looks like everything below my elbow got put on backwards, and it's all bloody." Tyler shakes his head.

"I know my arm's broken, but at least it's still attached, from what I can tell, anyway, so I'm thinking, 'Okay, at least I don't have to leave part of my arm here in this hellhole.' And then

I see I'm bleeding from my chest and my side too, like a lot. The red of the blood is like the only color I can see, while the rest of the world is brown and gray. And I get this weird, slow-motion sensation where I'm completely zeroed in on the blood leaving my body and seeping into the sand. It's so weird. In my head, I just hear the words 'blood and treasure, blood and treasure...'—you know, like the analysts on TV were always talking about all the *blood and treasure* the US spilled in Afghanistan. I can see my blood seeping into the sand, and I'm just thinking it's *my* blood now. My blood. It all sounds so abstract when you hear these experts talking on TV, right, but you can't ever understand what it's like to actually be surrounded by the blood that's being spilled. When it's your blood or the blood of people you know, your friends... It's, like, impossible to describe. That's what I think about the most, even now. How my blood looked when it was seeping into the dirty sand on this shitty road in some shitty place. And it was weird—I almost felt like... like no matter what happened now, I was leaving part of myself in this shitty country. I was always going to be connected to this place because of my blood being absorbed into the ground here. It was this crazy, existential-crisis moment right in the middle of a goddamn firefight." Tyler shakes his head. "Fucked-up, right?" he says without looking at me.

"I don't think it's fucked-up. Your brain is trying to cope with this trauma you were still right in the middle of," I say, clutching him a little tighter.

"Anyway, they get me loaded onto the helicopter, and they give me something that knocks me out, and the next thing I remember, I'm in the hospital, and they're pinning a purple heart on me. They patched up my chest and abdomen, but my arm needed more specialized surgery than they could handle. I think they kept me pretty drugged up for a while because all the memories I have of being in the hospital there are fuzzy. But I remember thinking they had stuffed cotton into my ears, and I couldn't figure out why they did that. But I decided that's why I couldn't hear properly, and I just went with that for a while. But a couple of days later, I started trying to pull out the cotton that of course wasn't there. They ended up writing down on a piece of paper that my hearing was damaged and I might not get it back."

"Anyway, so a while later, they flew me out, and I ended up at the VA hospital in Texas. I got the surgery and PT. And then, after that, they kinda... released me into the wild." Tyler snorts.

I barely know what to say. I move us so I can look at him and he can see my mouth. "Fuck, Tyler. I'm... I don't know what to say other than I'm so fucking sorry you had to go through that. I wish so much it hadn't happened to you."

"Thanks," he says. "It sucks, but I'm alive. I went through a phase where I wasn't so grateful for that, but thankfully, it didn't last long for me. But I understand how easy it would be to get to where you were angry that you hadn't died. It was just... so much..."

"Thank you for telling me," I say.

His eyes soften as he looks into mine and then leans in and places a gentle kiss on my mouth before moving so he's lying against me, his cheek resting on my chest. We lie quietly for a few moments, and I soothe both of us by running my fingers through his short dark hair. A short time later, his breathing evens out, and his body relaxes into sleep. Our breaths sync up, and he nuzzles into me, making sweet little snuffling noises. But I lie there for a long time, struggling to comprehend the things Tyler has lived through. It takes a long time before I've followed him, slipping into a fitful sleep.

CHAPTER 21

TYLER

I don't know what time it is when I slowly wake up, but the light from outside has that silvery, pre-dawn quality to it, telling me it's early. Slowly, I realize that the lovely warm body pillow I'm curled up against is an actual body. The events of last night come rushing back to me. My chest squeezes painfully when I recall how Sam held me so tenderly, letting me talk after helping me to calm down and get cleaned up after the nightmare. He didn't try to make it all better; he just held me and listened.

Lying quietly beside him, I feel his heartbeat against my cheek, and I love the way the rhythm of our breathing matches up. I reach over and grab my hearing aids, and then I doze off and on for a while until his breathing changes as he blinks slowly awake.

Tilting my head back so I can see his face but keeping our bodies in contact, I smile at his drowsy expression.

"Hi there."

"Hey," he replies. A flash of uncertainty crosses his face, but he relaxes when I lean in and place a soft kiss to the sliver of his collarbone not covered by his T-shirt. I'm in no hurry to put any distance between our bodies. "Are you... How are you feeling?" he asks.

Being this close to him means I can read his lips easily, but I can also feel the vibrations of his voice, and it sends warmth spreading through my chest. Waking up together in the same bed feels more intimate than anything else we've done, including hooking up that first night. Aside from the night of the storm with Sam, I haven't fallen asleep with anyone I've hooked up with since I lost my hearing. I've never been good at letting people get close to me, and since losing my hearing, there's not a chance of anyone getting in. Hookups have been few and far between in the last couple of years, and the rare times it has happened, it's always been at a loud bar, where the absolute minimum of conversation is required, and no way would I ever invite some random to come home with me.

"I'm feeling good," I say, realizing it's the truth. Even after the nightmare, I'm more rested than normal. "Thank you, Sam," I say softly, leaning back so I can see him. "Thank you for last night. Usually, I can't rest at all after a dream like that, but with you here, I slept. It feels good."

His brown eyes soften as he looks at me, sending a warm, comforting feeling through my chest. "Good. And I'm grateful you told me, Ty. It's probably not easy to talk about that day. So, thank you for sharing it with me. That means a lot to me."

His heart speeds up under my hand, and this strong feeling of clarity comes over me. I know beyond a shadow of a doubt that I can trust Sam. I don't know how, but I know it deep down in my bones.

I stretch up to kiss him, and the way he pulls me into him makes me feel like the most important thing in the universe, like I'm some kind of precious treasure.

I press closer to him still, and he slides his hands down to my ass, squeezing me and shifting us both so I'm on top of him, our hard cocks lined up, pressing against each other through the thin layers of our underwear.

"Too many clothes," I say against his mouth, and we both chuckle. Somehow, we manage to get our clothes off while barely taking our mouths off each other, and soon we're stretched out, skin to skin, and it's glorious.

His lips are soft but firm, leaving no doubt who's in charge. It's surprising, but I like it. I like turning over a little of my control to Sam. I trust him, and it's a major turn-on. We kiss for what seems like hours before he rolls us so I'm underneath him, the weight of his body anchoring me, pressing me into the soft bed and grounding me in this place and this time. Calmness spreads through me, even as my heartbeat speeds up. It's like Sam's big, strong body is sheltering me, blocking out the world so there's only his skin against mine and the delicious press of his lips and tongue. I'm safe. I'm home.

He thrusts against me, and I arch into him, my body craving more contact, more friction, more everything. He runs his tongue along the cord of my neck and places hot, open-mouthed kisses along my collarbone before shifting so he can suck first one nipple and then the other while sliding his hands all over my body.

Moving slowly, he makes his way down my torso, taking time to lick every inch of my abs and tonguing my belly button. He traces each one of my tattoos that cover most of my scars from the explosion, and when he encounters a patch of raised skin with his fingertips, he kisses it tenderly. His touch tickles, and I let out a breathy giggle. He looks up at me through his lashes, a playful smirk on his lips.

"Ticklish, are we?" he teases, then runs his fingers along my sides, a featherlight touch that makes me laugh and squirm. "Duly noted. That info will come in handy later." He stops tickling and continues working his way down my body with his mouth.

Finally, finally, when I think I might not last one more second, he makes his way to my aching cock, first pressing his nose against me and inhaling my scent.

"Saaam," I whine in a tone of voice I don't think I've ever used. "Pleeease..."

His only response is a devious look directed at me through his lashes, and I sigh in relief when I feel his hot breath against my skin. But just when I think he's finally going to put me out of my misery, he only licks a narrow stripe up one side of my dick and down the other. He teases me until I'm writhing against him, sure that I'm about to burst apart from want, before he finally takes me fully into his mouth in one smooth, slow motion. Sealing his lips tight around me, he sucks with steady pressure, moving his head slowly down my shaft and back up with a consistent rhythm.

"Oh god, Sam," I whisper, arching toward him, so desperate for more contact.

He wraps his hand around my base and moves it in tandem with his mouth, driving me out of my mind. He lets out a little moan of pleasure and pulls off just long enough to murmur, "Fuck, you taste so good," and sucks me back into his hot mouth. A shudder rolls through me, and I look down to find the corners of his eyes crinkled up, like he'd be teasing me if his mouth wasn't full of my dick.

Just when I think I'm not going to be able to hold out one more second, he pulls off me, causing me to gasp. He shoots me a devious smile as he licks and nibbles his way back up my body, taking time to pay special attention to each nipple on his way before finally making it back to my mouth.

I wrap my legs around his waist, pulling him as close as I can, undulating against him, trying to find more friction. He pulls back enough to grab my wrists, capturing them before pulling my arms above my head.

"Is this okay?" he asks, and I nod frantically.

"Yes, god yes, Sam. I need you inside me. Please. Supplies are in the drawer."

He lets go of my wrists and gives me a stern look that's so hot I almost blow then and there. "Leave your arms right there."

He reaches over and grabs the condom and lube out of the drawer in the bedside table, and I watch as he rolls it over himself. He slicks up his hands with lube first and then slides his fingers up and down his own erection, letting out a groan as he does. Once he's all slippery, he takes hold of my cock in one hand, stroking it slowly but firmly, and with the other hand, he runs his fingertips over my entrance. I gasp as he circles my hole with his slippery middle finger before slowly dipping inside me with just the tip. He pauses for just a moment to let my body adjust before sliding his finger inside a little further, driving me crazy with need. When I start to push against him, trying to drive his finger deeper, he smiles wickedly and releases my cock so he can take one of my legs and rest it over his shoulder, opening me wider to him, and then slides another finger into me beside the first. "Mmmm, so good for me," he says softly. "Look at you, keeping your hands just where I told you to. Such a good boy for me, Tyler."

Hearing him call me a good boy does something to me, and my desperation for him grows impossibly stronger. I whimper and thrash around under him, grabbing the sheets above my head as I fight to keep my hands where he told me to. "God, fuck, Sam... Please."

Unmoved by my begging, he pumps his fingers in and out of me, scissoring them and stretching me so slowly I'm not sure I'll survive it. My cock has never been so hard, and I'm starting to wonder if it's possible for a person to die from need when he finally slides his fingers out of me and shifts so his dick is lined up with my hole. I hold my breath as I feel him push against me, his cock so much bigger than his fingers, but oh my god, the stretch feels so good.

· · · • • • • • · ·

SAM

Tyler spread out beneath me, desperate and frantic with need, is the hottest thing I've ever seen. Hearing him beg for release and knowing I'm the only one who can give it to him makes me feel more powerful than I ever have, but it's mixed with my overwhelming need to protect him and care for him. His eyes are closed as I line my condom-covered cock up with his hole, but I want to see his eyes. "Look at me, Tyler," I command as I push just my cockhead into him before pausing to let his muscles adjust around me.

He snaps his eyes open, and the naked want in them nearly sends me over the edge. I have to close my own eyes for a second to calm myself down before pushing forward as slowly as I can manage until I'm fully seated inside him, my thighs pressed tightly against his ass. He trembles and rocks his hips, seeking more. "More, Sam. Fuck me, please..."

I pull back, keeping the pace excruciatingly slow, and slide back into him in one smooth movement, swallowing his desperate moans. "Sam, please, oh god, fuck, Sam."

He's almost crying with need when I finally pull back one more time before slamming my hips into him. He cries out as I fuck into his willing body fast and hard a few times before changing it up and leaning forward to take his mouth in a deep, hot kiss. I reach up and lace our fingers together above our heads. We're stretched out against each other, pressed tightly together from shoulders to hips as our bodies take over, instinctively finding the perfect rhythm. His cock rubs between our bellies, and I swear I can almost feel it grow harder as his movements against me become more erratic, and his breathing speeds up. He whimpers against my mouth, and I pull back so I can watch his face as he reaches his peak. "Come for me, Tyler. I want to feel you come on my cock." His breath catches as he tips over the edge, his entire body clenching and the muscles in his ass clamping down on my dick so hard it drags me right over with him. I want to keep watching his face as he falls, but I can't keep my eyes open as the orgasm overtakes me. I bury my head in the crook of his neck as we come at the same time, my vision whiting out for a few moments before I collapse against him, utterly spent.

As soon as I can move my limbs again, I shift off him so I don't crush him under me. Reaching down to the ground beside the bed, I find a discarded T-shirt and use it to clean us both off and then deal with the condom, tying it off to deal with later before gathering Tyler in my arms, loving the way his body melts into mine.

"You're incredible," I murmur to him, not even sure whether he can hear me but unable to stop whispering sweet nothings to him before we both drift back to sleep.

CHAPTER 22

TYLER

The rest of the weekend goes by like a dream. Sam and I barely leave the bed, and it's pretty much the best fucking thing I've ever experienced in my life. Pun fully intended. In between orgasms and sleeping, we drink a couple of bottles of wine, grill steaks again, and generally get to know each other even better. I don't want to stop to examine how amazing Sam makes me feel. Once again, I put a pin in it, telling myself I'll examine it later.

Late Sunday afternoon, we decide to head down to the beach for a walk. I've been neglecting my sketchbook for the last couple of days, having had much more interesting things to think about, but I grab it as we're walking out the door, and when we stop for a few minutes to let the last watery rays of sunlight warm us before heading back to the cabin, I sketch a very quick drawing of Sam's profile. I don't hide it from him, although when he asks if he can see it, I shyly shake my head. I promise him I'll show him when I'm finished tinkering with it, and he seems to be satisfied with that answer.

By the time Sunday night rolls around, we're tired from all the fresh air and the orgasms, and we cuddle in bed, falling asleep without even having sex. It's so natural to fall asleep in Sam's arms that I didn't notice the absence of anything. I feel like Sam fills a hole in my soul that I didn't even know was there, which might be the cheesiest, most ridiculous sentence ever, but it's true.

Monday morning, we're up early. Sam slides out of bed before me, so he makes the coffee. Afterward, we head over to the main building and continue work.

Our working relationship stays completely the same. Casual, comfortable, and easy. We tease and flirt and banter back and forth in a way that's become natural for us. I've loved working at Hot Dam Homes from the beginning, but working with Sam is just... fun.

As the week passes, we slide further into this domestic routine of eating together, cleaning up, snuggling for a while, and then crawling into bed at the same time. It turns out Sam's more than happy to go to bed early with me. He reads or plays a quiet game on his phone if he's not tired, but he always holds me in his arms until I fall asleep. Again, not wanting to look too hard at how good that feels.

We take advantage of a few unseasonably warm winter days and go for walks on the beach in the afternoon before it gets too dark, finishing up whatever we're working on in the early evening. Toward the end of the week, the weather returns to normal, with rain and wind battering the buildings and turning the worksite into a muddy pit.

It's midafternoon on Friday when Sam texts me from the other room that he's got a bunch of stuff to go out to the dumpster. It's a job we both hate since getting stuff out there involves going down some stairs and negotiating a muddy, uneven path with a full wheelbarrow, so we decided to take turns.

I throw my own pile of trash into the wheelbarrow and then take it into the room where Sam's working. Once we've loaded it, he grabs me around the waist, pulling me close and planting a kiss on me that I can feel all the way down to my toes.

When he releases me, we're both breathless and laughing.

"Sorry," Sam chuckles. "That's probably inappropriate fraternizing between coworkers. I'll try to keep my hands to myself, but I've been waiting to do that all day."

I laugh. "It's okay. I promise not to file a complaint against you." I waggle my eyebrows, and he rolls his eyes.

"How do you feel about going into town for dinner tonight?" he asks. "We haven't really gotten out much for the past few days..." He trails off and grins evilly.

"Works for me," I say, and he turns back to his task while I lift the handles and head for the door. I get out to the porch when the cell phone in my pocket starts to vibrate. When I see the call is coming from my mother's care home, my chest gets tight, and my stomach roils unpleasantly.

I hold up my phone and quickly bring up the live caption service built into it. It's a cool feature that tells the person calling you that you're using captioning. I don't always use it, but when it's something important, I find it helpful.

"This is Tyler Ritchie," I speak into the phone clearly and wait for the computer to transcribe what the person on the other end says. A few seconds later, the words come up on my phone screen, and my stomach clenches painfully.

"Oh. Um. Hello, Mr. Ritchie? My name is Jericka, and I'm calling from Tall Firs Care Home. It's regarding Ms. Shelly Ritchie."

"Shelly Ritchie is my mother. Is there a problem?" I say and then wait for the transcription to appear. I'm frozen in place, waiting to see what the fuck is happening with my mother.

"Yes, um, okay. Well, unfortunately, Ms. Ritchie had a fall earlier today, and we've had to take her to the hospital. We've left a message for a Mr. Aaron Ritchie, but it's been a few hours, and we haven't heard back from him, and your name is next on the contact list."

The blood in my veins turns to ice when I read the words. *Fuck, fuck,* fuck. I have to ask the question.

"Okay. Ah. Is it serious? I'm, um… I'm out of town right now. Do I need to come back?" I know asking that question makes me sound like an absolute asshole, but these people don't know the heavy history of our family. They don't know or care that my mother left my brother and me alone for most of our childhood, forcing us to raise ourselves.

There's a slightly longer than normal pause before I see the words come across my screen that make up her response, so obviously she hesitated, probably a little shocked by the question.

"Ah. Well, of course, we can't make that decision for anyone. Um. But my personal opinion is that you might want to try to get here. Ms. Ritchie has had some other health issues recently. She's quite frail, and these types of falls can cause a lot of other issues."

I grit my teeth and have to stop myself from swearing like a sailor at the poor woman on the phone. It figures. I'm having most amazing time of my life, floating on a high like I've never had before, spending time with an amazing man who makes me feel like the most important person on the planet, and my asshole of a mother swoops in to take one more thing away from me.

"Okay, ah, I'll make arrangements to get there sometime tonight. Which hospital is she in?" Jericka gives me the information, and the hand not holding my phone clenches into a fist. I feel like slamming it into a wall.

Motherfucker. I close my eyes and blow out a long breath, and when I open them, Sam is walking toward me, looking concerned.

"Ty, is everything okay? I thought I heard you talking out here."

"I'm fine." I let out a frustrated sigh. "I have to go into Tacoma right away."

"Huh? Why?" Sam asks.

"My mother's care home called. She fell today, and she's in the hospital. I guess it's pretty bad since the woman from the home thought I should get there as soon as I can."

"Oh, no. And your brother?"

"I guess they tried calling him first, but they haven't heard back yet."

"I'm sorry, Tyler," Sam says, reaching out to wrap his arms around me. I don't let myself sink into him like I usually do though. My brain is already going a million miles an hour, and I have to get moving.

"Yeah, I'm sorry too. This fucking sucks," I mutter, feeling like a petulant child.

"Okay," he says, pausing for a second to think. "I'll drive you. Why don't you have a shower while I call Mase and tell him you've got a family emergency. There's already gas in the truck, so we won't have to stop other than to maybe grab some fast food or something along the way."

"Wait, you don't have to..." I start to protest Sam driving me into Tacoma, but I stop when he shoots me a look that brooks no argument.

"I'm coming with you. I promise not to hover over you, but I'm driving you."

Whoa. I kind of like this "take-charge" version of Sam Campbell. Even though it's not exactly the ideal circumstances. He's a little bossy in the bedroom, which I find incredibly hot, but this commanding attitude he has right now is a definite turn-on.

"Okay. I'm sorry for the hassle," I say, letting out a huge sigh.

He steps closer to me and snakes his arm around my waist, grabbing my chin and turning my face toward his.

"Do not apologize, please. I want to help you. Okay?" he says, his eyes searching mine.

"Okay. Thank you," I say, swallowing hard as his eyes bore into mine. He plants a firm kiss on my mouth before releasing me, and we walk quickly back to the guest cabin.

I jump into the shower, alone with my thoughts, while Sam fusses around getting stuff ready to go. It sounds like my mom is in bad shape, and I don't know how to feel about it. My feelings about her are so complicated. I'm also nervous about what I'll find when I get to her. Will she be openly hostile to me—will she even know me? She often doesn't. And what should I do about Sam? Should I bring him with me when I see her? I don't really want him to see the abuse she sometimes hurls at me. And then there's the situation with Aaron. One of us is going to have to sack up and confront the tension between us. Fuck, it's just too much right now. I can hear Derek's voice in my head. *One thing at a time, Tyler.*

I finish up in the shower, drying off as quickly as possible. I have no idea how I'm going to handle any of this, but it appears the only way out of it is through.

CHAPTER 23

SAM

While Tyler showers, I run around and lock up the main building, then throw a few things into an overnight bag for each of us and load them into the truck. I text Mason and let him know what's happening, and he responds, telling me not to worry about work, to just make sure Tyler is doing okay and to keep him posted.

Once we get into the truck and start heading for Tacoma, a weird silence descends upon us. I'm sure Tyler is worried about his mom, but he doesn't say much about it. As much as I want to push him for information so I can know the right ways to help him feel better, I force myself to leave him alone. He probably needs some time to process what's happening.

"Any word from your brother yet?" I ask after we've been driving for a while.

Tyler nods. "Yeah, I texted with him. He booked a flight from Nashville for tomorrow." He lets his head fall back and blows out a long sigh. "I haven't seen Aaron in over two years," he says without opening his eyes.

"Oh," I say, trying to keep the shock out of my voice. He had said he wasn't as close with his brother as he used to be, but I didn't realize they were basically estranged. "Because of the argument you had?" I ask.

Tyler nods. "Yeah. I feel like it's a lot more my fault than Aaron's."

"What makes you think that?" I ask gently. "In my experience, it usually takes two people to have a fight."

"I told Aaron he should be the one who shouldered the burden of our mother's care since he never bothered to join the military and got to sit home on his ass while I went over and defended our country." Tyler sighs. "Basically, I called him a coward, and I feel like shit about it. I'd been drinking, and I was so fucking confused and angry about what happened to me that I barely knew which end was up."

I reach out to take Tyler's hand. "I think that's understandable, Ty. You'd just been through a serious trauma, and you weren't even physical-ly healed yet, let alone mentally."

"Yeah, but he got screwed over too. He had to put his dreams on hold, first for me to finish high school and then again when he had to haul ass back here so he could take care of our hor-rible mother, who would have never done the same for us. And to make things even worse for Aaron, he found out right before that fight that our mom had stolen his social security number and racked up a shit-ton of debt in his name."

"Holy shit, that's fucking awful." God, the more I hear about this woman, the more I wish I could go back in time and kick her ass.

"Yeah, it's not great. She's so fucked-up, Sam. And I was such a mess back then it's embar-rassing to even think about it." He pauses for a minute, but I wait, sensing he's not finished talking. "Understandably, Aaron was pissed. He started yelling that I was nothing but a burden to him and I was turning out to be the same as our mother since I was drinking all the fucking time. That nearly killed me."

"Oh, Tyler, I'm sorry," I say. "It sounds like you were both in a really bad place."

"Yeah. That's an understatement. I'd lost my hearing but was too stubborn to go to the VA to get hearing aids and the other therapy I needed. I was just avoiding my problems, looking for the answers in a bottle, the same way she always did." He shakes his head.

"After that blowout, I pulled my head out of my ass and started seeing Derek for help with the PTSD. Then I was able to get my hearing aids, and things started going better, but my relationship with Aaron never recovered. We both apologized, and it's okay on the surface, but we haven't ever talked about the things we said. And we haven't seen each other in person since that fight. Some things are hard to take back, you know? But I miss him."

Tyler blows out a heavy breath and stares out the window. "I was so angry at the time. God, part of the reason I got help was just to spite him, to prove him wrong. But I get it now. He was right about me. I was heading down that same path as our mother. When I think about it now, it scares the shit out of me." Tyler shakes his head, and I squeeze his hand, unsure what to say that might help. Maybe there's nothing I can say. Maybe he just needs me to listen. His story is hitting that button inside me that makes me want to step in and protect him though, and it's hard not to go off on a rant about what a terrible parent his mom was. But I don't think that's what he needs.

"I just wish I'd been able to deal with my shit even a tiny bit better. I could have made things so much easier on Aaron. I got off lucky—my credit wasn't affected by our mom's stunt. I've been helping Aaron to pay off her debt. But our relationship hasn't been the same since that fight."

"God, Tyler, I'm so sorry. But I know how strong you are. I don't think you would have gone down that same path as your mom, I really don't. But even if you had, you wouldn't be in the same situation because you were in a bad place due to injuries, physical and PTSD. And I believe you would have been able to find your way out of it." God, I can't imagine what it would be like to grow up with a parent like that. I send out a silent thank-you to the universe for my family.

"Maybe you and Aaron needed some time to pass before you talked. Maybe this will be a chance for you two to work things out if that's what you want," I say, trying to give him a little hope.

He gives me a slightly empty smile. "Maybe," he says softly. "I guess we'll find out soon." He turns back to the window, staring out at the dark as we get closer to the city.

CHAPTER 24

TYLER

The knot in my stomach grows heavier the closer we get to the city. I thought opening up to Sam about things between Aaron and me might get rid of the aching tension in my belly, but thinking about those awful days right after getting home doesn't do much to calm me down. God, I'd been such a mess, and until I started seeing Derek, my psychiatrist, Aaron was the only person I really saw, so he bore the brunt of all my grief and rage.

"So, we're getting close," Sam says after I've been silent for a while, and I'm jolted out of my thoughts to find we're stopped at a light a few blocks from the hospital.

"Oh, yeah, it's right up there. I think the main entrance is on the right. You can just drop me off at the door there," I say, but then I realize we haven't discussed what's happening now. Is Sam planning to turn around and head back to the coast? Or head home to Seattle? Or is he planning to stick around with me? I don't know what I want him to do. The thought of bringing him to see my mom makes the bile rise in the back of my throat. It's one thing to tell him about her and my life growing up, but it's entirely something else to have him meet her.

Before I can figure it out, Sam pulls into a "10 minute only" parking spot.

"Sit right there for a second," he commands, and my god, he's sexy when he gives orders.

He jumps out of the truck and comes to my side, opening the door for me. As soon as my feet hit the ground, he wraps me in his strong arms for a hug.

"You go in and find your mom, see if you can talk to a doctor or someone tonight. I'll go check us into a decent hotel and get settled. Text me when you want me to come pick you up, okay?"

"Yeah, okay. That sounds good. I'll text you soon." Relief that Sam is taking control of the logistics while my mind is so scrambled washes over me.

"I'll be here when you're ready," he says. He kisses me tenderly on the forehead, and I head toward the entrance. I pull my jacket close around me. How is it that it feels colder here than it does out on the coast?

I walk into the hospital, and even though it's only just after dinnertime on a Friday night, there aren't many people around. Thankfully, there's a lady with short, white hair and glasses sitting at the reception desk. She smiles at me as I approach. After I give my mother's name, she checks my ID, gives me a visitor pass, and directs me to the fourth floor.

It feels like there's a lead weight in my gut as the elevator rises. I have no idea what I'm going to find there. Sometimes my mother can be physically violent, sometimes she's verbally abusive, and other times she's quiet and docile. I don't know what to expect.

Once I'm on the right ward, a nurse directs me to a room at the far end of one of the dimly lit hallways. I guess it's lights-out early for these folks.

Taking a deep breath, I square my shoulders and walk into the hospital room. It's not a private room; there are four people in there, and to my surprise, there's a mix of both men and women. Strange—I didn't know hospital rooms were co-ed. I have to look at each person twice before I recognize my mother, and I can't help the gasp that escapes me when I realize the tiny, shrunken form lying motionless in the bed furthest away from the door is her. On Jell-O-like legs, I take a few steps closer to the bed to make sure, but yes, it's definitely my mother. To be honest, she hasn't looked like my mom for a few years, not since she's been in the care home, but now she looks like... I don't know... some kind of... elf or hobbit or something. She was always a small person, but she's barely bigger than a child now. One of her arms is in a cast up to her armpit. There's a white gauze bandage on her forehead that might need to be changed since the dark patch on it shows she's been bleeding underneath it. The skin around her eyes is such a dark purple it's nearly black with the double shiners she's sporting. I can't see what's going on underneath her blankets, but it looks like she has a cast on one of her legs as well. Her mouth is slightly open, and she's breathing shallowly.

She's attached to an IV and a heart rate monitor, which beeps softly as I stand there staring.

Jesus fucking Christ. How the hell do you do that much damage from a simple fall? My mother is only in her fifties, but she looks closer to eighty years old right now.

I'm still standing at the foot of her bed, dumbfounded, when a nurse comes bustling into her area.

"Oh, well, hi there!" she says in a cheerful voice. I've got my hearing aids turned up, so even though she's not looking at me, I can hear her. "My name's Tonya. You're here to visit Miss Shelly?"

"Um, yes," I stammer. "I'm, um. Her son. I'm her son. One of her sons."

"Oh, that's nice." She fusses around my mother's bed for a moment, checking one of the machines she's hooked up to and then putting two fingers on my mother's wrist and glancing at her watch while she gets the vital signs. She smiles at me when she's finished and then types some notes into the tablet that's attached to my mother's bed. "I always like to double-check these machines by doing it the old-fashioned way when I have time," she says with a wink. She's got an accent that I can both hear and see in her mouth movements. Maybe from some-where in the South?

Given that the rooms are dark, and it seems like most of the patients, in this room at least, are down for the night, it doesn't seem like I'll be able to talk to a doctor tonight. Tonya is probably going to have more info than anyone else right now.

"Um, is it, can we, can I—can I talk to you about her?" I ask, feeling like a fool. I don't know the etiquette for these kinds of situations. Can a nurse pass information to me, or does everything have to come through the doctor? I haven't got a clue.

"Of course, honey," she says with a kind smile. "Come with me so we don't wake anyone in here."

I follow her out of the room and down the hall to the nurses' station, where she takes a seat behind the desk and looks up at me.

"I'm not sure how much you've been told by your mother's care home, but I can tell you what I know."

I nod.

"She came in earlier today, after spending a few hours in the emergency department. According to her file, she had an altercation with another resident at the care home." Tonya clears her throat and squints at the screen she's reading from. "Apparently, she pushed another resident down a flight of stairs, but the other person grabbed her and pulled her with them, so they both fell. Seems like your momma took the brunt of it, though, as the other person was treated here but was released."

"Oh, fuck," I say without thinking, and then I'm immediately embarrassed. "Oh my god, I'm sorry." Tonya waves off my apology, and I clear my throat. "God, she... she pushed someone down the stairs? That's how this happened?"

She gives me another kind look. "I don't know any more than that, but I see here that your mom has advanced dementia?"

I nod.

"So, I know it's hard, but try to remember that these kinds of issues are real common for people struggling with that. It's a terrible disease. You have to remember it's not really her that's doing all these out-of-character things. The behavior, especially the violence, that's her illness talking, not your momma."

I nod. This is stuff I've heard before, but until now, I haven't had to face the fact that her condition has gotten so bad she's able to hurt people—herself included. "Um, do you... Can you tell me what injuries she has?"

Tonya looks down at the screen and starts reading off a list. After about five things, I start to tune out. I barely know what any of it means, but suffice it to say that my mother is seriously fucked-up.

I'm not sure what to say, and I have no idea what to do next. It must be painfully obvious because Tonya stands and puts her warm hand over top of mine where it's resting on the desk. She gives me a squeeze. "I don't think I got your name, honey. What's your name?" she asks.

"Tyler," I mumble.

"Okay, Tyler. I know this is a lot to take in, especially if you haven't seen her for a while. Alzheimer's is a real bitch—it steals the people we love right out from under us. I wish I had some better news to share about your mom, but right now, that's all I've got. She's stable, and we're taking good care of her. The doctor will be in tomorrow. He's usually here around mid-morning to do rounds. You should be able to talk to him then. You can also try the care home people since they're the authorized guardians in your absence. But right now, I think you should go home or back to wherever you're staying tonight and try to get some sleep."

"Right... Yeah. That's what I'll do. Right," I mumble again, and I'm sure Tonya must think I'm having some kind of breakdown because I can barely string together two words. "I'll. Um. I'll be back tomorrow. In the morning. Tomorrow morning."

Tonya smiles and nods. "That's a good idea. I'm on shift until 7:00 a.m., but I'll be back tomorrow evening if you're here again. And Crystal is on the day shift—you'll like her. She's lovely, and she'll take good care of your momma."

"Okay. Right. Thanks. Yeah. I'll see you tomorrow, then," I say, turning to head toward the elevator.

I somehow make my way down to the main floor and outside, where I collapse on a bench just outside the emergency room doors. I sit there for a few minutes, trying to absorb what I've just seen and heard. First of all, she's hurt, like, badly hurt. And who knows how long she's going to have to be in the hospital. Second of all, she's now become so violent that she's attacking other patients at her care home.

Finally, I pull myself together enough to text Sam that I'm ready. The hotel is close by, so in less than ten minutes, I'm climbing into the white pickup with the cute Hot Dam Homes beaver logo on the door. It's fucking insane that only a few hours ago, I was happier than I could ever remember being in my life, and then the shoe drops. *Typical.*

"Hey there," Sam says when I get in the truck. "How is she? Did you learn anything?"

"Not much," I lie. I can't face the truth right now. And I can't face the way Sam is going to look at me. The way he's going to pity me when he realizes the shitshow my life is. Fuck. I don't want him to have to put up with this kind of crap. It's not fair. This is my mess to deal with, not his.

"I need to go back to the hospital tomorrow morning to talk with the doctor. I'll learn more then." I stare out the window as Sam drives us through the seedier part of town and into the nicer area where he's found a decent hotel.

We're quiet until we get to our room, and I'm grateful for him getting taking care of everything. The bed looks big and comfortable, and I'm so goddamn exhausted I feel like an extra from *The Walking Dead*, but I need to get out of my head for a while. And I know of one surefire way to make that happen.

I turn to Sam as soon as the door to the room closes behind us, launching myself at him. His eyes grow wide with surprise as I attack him with my mouth, desperately biting his lips and ripping at his shirt, trying to get as close to him as I can.

"Hey, hey—are you alright?" He pulls back slightly and looks into my eyes.

"No," I say simply. The truth feels good. "I need you to help me get out of my head for a little while, Sam. Please?"

His eyes darken as he looks at me, like he's thinking about it, wondering if this is a good idea, fucking me while I'm clearly upset. "Please, Sam. I need to get away from my thoughts for a bit. Please." My voice breaks as he holds my face between his hands, looking at me with the utmost seriousness.

"You tell me to stop and we stop, no matter what, okay? No questions asked, we'll stop."

I nod, throwing myself at him again, clawing and begging. "Yes, I promise I'll tell you if I need to stop. Just... I need... I need you to take over for a while... Sam, please..."

"Okay, it's okay, babe. I'm here," he says in a gentle voice.

CHAPTER 25

SAM

Oh, fuck. Does he mean what it sounds like? Because it sounds like Tyler wants me to take control of *everything* for a little while, and that thought makes me swallow hard as blood rushes south to my dick.

"You're sure, Ty? I just want to be clear... You want me to be in charge? Tell you what to do and when?"

His cheeks flush bright pink, and his eyes drop, embarrassed. "Yeah. I just want to feel, not think."

My heart is pounding, but I know I need answers before we do anything. I've played around with kink a little, but it's been a long time. I'm also keenly aware that Tyler's incredibly vulnerable at the moment, but I want to give him what he needs if there's any way I can.

"Okay, babe, we need to talk for a second first." I lead him to the edge of the bed, where we sit down. "I need you to tell me what you're thinking. Exactly what you want to try. We have to make sure we're on the same page."

Tyler looks down at his hands for a moment before he shifts his gaze to me. His voice is steady and strong when he speaks. "I know what I'm asking for, Sam. I need you to... I want you to be in charge. I want you to control me. Control everything I feel. I want to feel pleasure when you want me to, pain when you want me to. I want you to tell me when I can come. I want you to be in charge."

Holy shit. I swallow hard. Yup, he means what it sounds like. "Okay, Ty. We can do that. But we need a safe word. I need to be sure I'm not going too far. Do you want to use the traffic light system? You say red to get me to stop, yellow to slow down, and green means you're good."

He nods eagerly. "Yeah, I can do that. I just need to get away from everything in my head."

"I know, babe," I say, caressing his cheek lightly. "I'll help you forget everything for a bit. I promise, baby." I place a firm, strong kiss on him. I search his eyes for a moment, looking for fear or reluctance, but all I see is hunger and desire.

"Okay, Tyler. First, I want you to stand and take your clothes off for me. Slowly."

He sucks in a breath, and his pupils dilate. "Okay," he says in a breathy voice and immediately stands up and peels off his T-shirt. "Will you undress too? Please?" he asks almost shyly.

"Is that what you want, baby?" I ask, and he nods. "Well, only because you asked me so nicely. I like hearing that word from your mouth." My voice sounds gravelly. I stand and start taking my own clothes off.

Once we're both undressed, he looks at me expectantly, waiting for me to give him his next instructions. I take a breath. I can do this. Fuck, I want this; but my heart is pounding so hard I'm surprised he can't hear it, hearing-impaired or not.

"Get down on your knees, Tyler. I want your mouth." I sit on the bed, my ass close to the edge and my legs spread, while he kneels before me. He shuffles closer so he's in between my knees, his hands on my thighs. He looks up at me again, and I nod. "Take me in your mouth. Suck me."

He opens and leans in toward my rock-hard dick as it strains toward him. He suckles gently on my tip, swirling his tongue around it before opening wide and taking me as far down as he can. I let out a groan at the feeling of his hot mouth surrounding me. God, he's incredible. He sucks me hard, his head bobbing up and down in a regular rhythm that causes my eyes to roll back in my head. The sight of him kneeling for me is so hot I could come just from watching him suck me off, but there's no way I'm going to let this end quickly. I'm surprised at how turned on I am from being in control of his pleasure. He trusts me to get him to that place where he doesn't have to think, and it's like an aphrodisiac. Knowing how few people Tyler truly trusts only makes it more special.

I card my fingers through his hair as he works me over, and I savor his moans as he swallows my precum. His mouth is so hot and wet, the suction perfect. His hands grip my thighs so hard I'm sure there will be finger-shaped bruises there tomorrow. I fucking love it. Throwing my head back, I groan his name as he takes me deep into his throat and swallows. The muscles constrict around me, and I nearly lose it. I touch his cheek to get his attention. "Stop," I gasp.

He pulls back immediately, and I encircle the base of my cock with my fingers, squeezing hard. It takes everything I have not to blow right there. "You're doing so good, Tyler. You've almost got me coming already," I pant.

He sits back on his heels and wipes his mouth with the back of his hand. His eyes are hooded, the pupils blown out, and his lips are puffy from stretching around me. Fuck, he looks so good.

I need him like I've never needed anything. Standing, I pull him to his feet and take his mouth in a blistering hot kiss. His moans and whimpers only add fuel to my overwhelming need for him as we rut against each other, our hard-as-steel cocks lining up perfectly. I break us apart, both of us gasping for air.

"On the bed, Tyler. On your knees, head on the pillow, ass up." I don't know where this version of me is coming from, but I have to admit I like how I sound. Tyler does too, his eyes flaring as he sucks in a breath and scrambles onto the bed to do as I ask.

Standing behind him, I admire his perfect ass, running my palms over his feverishly hot skin. "God, you're beautiful," I breathe before spreading his cheeks and leaning in, pressing my face into him, and inhaling. Fuck, he even smells good. Earthy and musky and so masculine. I can't stop the groan that escapes me. "Fuck." I whisper to myself before running my tongue the length of his crack. He gasps, which brings a smile to my face.

"Tyler, have you ever done this before? Ever let someone see you like this? Taste you this way?"

A shudder runs through him as he shakes his head.

"N-n-n -no... Never." His voice is ragged. He's as wrecked as I am.

"So, I'm the first one who gets to have you like this?" I ask.

He nods.

"I need your words, Tyler. I need to hear you," I breathe.

"Yeah... Y-yes. You're the only one, Sam."

"Mmm," I murmur. "So good." I pull him apart and lean back in, licking and sucking until he's writhing under me, moaning my name. I dip my tongue into him, and he jerks forward with a gasp but then immediately presses back into me, seeking more.

All the blood in my body feels like it's concentrated in my dick, which is throbbing painfully.

I keep at him, plunging my tongue into him over and over until I feel him soften for me. *Jesus fuck*, I hope I can last.

"I'm going to give you my fingers now, baby. You want that?"

He groans; I think he's lost the ability to speak.

He whimpers as I pull away from him for a moment to grab the supplies out of my bag and slick up my fingers. When I return, I lean over him, my chest to his back, and pull his earlobe into my mouth, sucking gently while I slide one finger gently into him. His muscles tense for a moment but quickly relax, letting me slide in another one and then one more finger, stretching him as he moans and fucks back against me.

Fuck, I feel so powerful, completely in charge of his pleasure like this. I never knew it could be so hot, taking over this way. I love it.

"God, you're so good, so hot, Tyler. I love the way your ass takes my fingers. I think you're almost ready for my cock, yeah? I whisper right into his ear, and he nods frantically.

"Fuck, yes. More. Please," he begs, and fuck if that doesn't almost catapult me right over the edge.

I pull my fingers out of him and quickly roll the condom on.

"Lie on your back, Tyler. Pull your legs up for me," I say, and he rushes to get situated, his head on the pillow. He holds himself open, and I let my eyes slide over him slowly. He's gorgeous this way. Wrecked and desperate for me. I kneel on the bed and shuffle forward until my cock is lined up directly with his entrance.

"You ready, baby?" I whisper, and he nods, desperation dripping off him like the beads of sweat dripping down his neck. I push forward into him and stop, both of us gasping, letting his body adjust. After a moment, I pull back a bit, then push in again a bit further, and his eyes roll back into his head. I feel the ring of muscle inside him give way, and I slide all the way inside him, my thighs pressed against his ass.

"Oh, god," he cries and grips my forearms as I pull back and slam into him again. His channel is so tight and hot around me I don't know if I can hold off, but he has to come first. I fall forward onto him, taking his mouth in a filthy kiss as I find my rhythm, sliding deep inside him over and over. I grab his cock, jerking him in time with my thrusts until I feel him begin to clench around me.

"Look at me, Tyler," I command, and his eyes snap open. His mouth opens in a silent scream as he comes, hot stripes of cum painting his chest. His ass clenches around my length, and I unload into the condom as we stare into each other's eyes until I can no longer hold myself up. I collapse beside him, utterly spent.

We lie together, breathing heavily as we recover. His eyes are still closed when I reach over and run my fingers through the cum pooled on his chest. He opens his eyes, looking sex drunk and hot as fuck. I bring my fingers to his mouth. His eyes widen, and he sucks in a breath.

"Open, baby. I want you to taste," I say, and a moan escapes him as I push my fingers inside. He sucks them greedily before I pull them out and scoop up a little more, bringing my hand to my own mouth this time. I revel in the taste of him, so goddamn sexy. This is the hottest experience of my life already, and we're just getting started.

CHAPTER 26

SAM

I blink awake slowly, and it takes me a minute to orient myself. Right. I'm in a hotel in Tacoma, and Tyler is nestled in beside me, sleeping like a baby, his head resting on my chest and his arm wrapped tightly around my midsection. Waking up with him pressed up against me like this is one of the best things I've ever experienced. I glance over at the old-school alarm clock on the bedside table, and its red analog numbers read 6:07 a.m. Still early. Tyler won't need to get up to go to the hospital for a few hours, and I want him to get as much sleep as he can. He didn't tell me much last night, but it doesn't sound like things are good, and I figure he's going to need all his strength to deal with whatever's coming at him.

Last night was the thing I've ever experienced. Don't get me wrong, I've always loved sex, and I've played a little with bossing people around in bed, but not much, and *nothing* like what we did last night. Oh. My. God. I've never come so hard in my life. I don't understand how I knew, but I knew right down to my bones that what Tyler needed last night wasn't lovemaking. It wasn't tender and sweet. He wanted to get out of his own head. He wanted to not have to think at all, only to feel. Taking charge of everything, including his pleasure, was a huge turn-on. It was incredible, and seeing how turned on he was only heightened the experience. I've never imagined that would be something I'd enjoy, but holy shit, enjoy it I did. A shiver runs down my spine, and my dick is all of a sudden a lot harder than my usual morning wood. I don't think I'd want sex to be like that every time, but holy fuck, it was so hot I'm surprised the paint didn't peel right off the walls of the hotel room.

I let my eyes drift closed again, allowing myself to float around in that half-awake, half-asleep state that can be so pleasant when you know you've got some time before you need to be out of bed.

Part of me wants nothing more than to just stay in this bed for the entire day, plundering Tyler's gorgeous body and discovering a whole lot more about what else turns us both on. But he said last night he had to get up early so he could meet the doctor, plus I'm antsy. I slide carefully out of bed and quietly get dressed in the bathroom. I'll go grab us some coffee and pastries from the Starbucks in the hotel lobby. I'm not sure whether Tyler will want me to go with him to the hospital or not, but I'll be there for whatever he needs from me.

It only takes a short time to get our stuff from the coffee shop, and I'm hoping he's still asleep in bed when I get back so I can kiss him awake. But unfortunately, he's standing in the bathroom, brushing his teeth when I walk in. He's showered already, as he's wearing only a towel around his waist and his hair is damp.

"Hey, I was kind of hoping you'd still be sleeping." I smile at him. "I wanted to give you an unforgettable wake-up call." He huffs a laugh, and I grin. "But since that didn't work out, I brought us breakfast."

"Oh, yeah, thanks," he says, his mouth full of toothpaste. He doesn't meet my eyes, just keeps puttering around at the bathroom counter, which is a little strange, but I ignore it and place the bag of scones and muffins on the little table beside the window with our coffees.

"So, what time would you like to head over to the hospital?" I ask when he comes out of the bathroom.

"Um, as soon as possible. I need to catch the doctor, and he could be there early. "

"Okay," I say. "I don't want to assume any-thing, but I was thinking if you didn't want me to hang out with you at the hospital today, I'll—"

"Um, yeah, about that, Sam," he interrupts me, and my stomach clenches. "My brother texted me earlier. He'll be here this afternoon. I'll stay at his place while we're dealing with this stuff, so you can probably head out after you drop me off at the hospital."

I stare at him for a second, shocked. Is he telling me to get the fuck out? No, that can't be right. Is he embarrassed about last night or something? But Tyler's not actually looking at me; he's turned around, and without taking the towel off, he slides his underwear on under-

neath it so I can't see anything while he's changing. It sounds stupid, but after the last week, and
especially after last night... him not wanting me
to see his ass while he gets dressed is just... it
hurts.

"Ooookaay?" I say, trying hard not to freak
out. Have I seriously done it again? Fucking
fallen for someone who doesn't feel the same
way? And holy shit, have I fallen for Tyler? *God-
damnit.*

Tyler lets out a sigh, and he looks as guilty
as one of those dogs wearing the signs that say
"I ate the shoes." Suddenly I'm hit with it like
a thunderbolt. *I'm being a total asshole.* I'm trying to make this situation about me, when it
has nothing to do with me. Tyler's mother is
seriously sick, he doesn't even know what her
prospect for recovery is, and he's got a brother
he isn't on great terms with to handle. *Pull your
head out of your ass, Sam. Not everything is about
you.*

"Sam, I just, I think it might be easier if I just
stay with Aaron, and we're going to have our
hands so full with everything..."

I shake my head and hold up my hand. "Tyler,
you don't have to explain. I get it. You've got
a lot going on. I understand. I don't want to

crowd you, but I want you to know I'll be here for anything you need."

The look on his face is unmistakably relieved, still mixed with guilt, but he closes his eyes for a brief second before talking. "Thank you so much. I think I'll be fine. Aaron should be getting in around lunchtime, but if something weird happens, it won't be a big deal for me to grab an Uber and head to his house. He said his landlord has the key and I can pick it up from them."

I nod. "Okay. Whatever you need, I can do, okay?"

He gives me another watery smile before turning back around to finish grabbing the few things he needs to throw into his bag.

Even though there's a voice inside me screaming at me to hold on tight, to not let him go, to make sure he knows I can be anything, do anything he needs, I manage to beat it back. He told me he needs space. I can give him space. This is probably partly what Jess meant when she said I tried to twist myself into whatever I thought she wanted.

It only takes me a few minutes to grab my own things from around the room, and after a superfast shower, we're walking across the parking lot to the truck.

When we get to the hospital, there's a slightly awkward pause when I pull up to the main entrance to drop him off, but I decide to take charge. Hmmm—it seems like taking charge is something I'm rather fond of...

"Okay, Tyler," I say, and I reach over the console to grab one of his hands, which are cold and clammy from the damp morning air. "Will you let me know how things are going? I'll try not to hover over you, but—"

"Of course I will," he interrupts. He looks up at me from underneath his lashes, which sounds like it should look ridiculous, but he pulls it off. I don't even think he's trying to look sweet; it's a natural thing. "As soon as I have a better idea of when I can come back to work, I'll let you and Mason know, but I'll keep you posted too."

"Okay," I say, and I have to bite my tongue not to add anything else. But this new, more confident version of Sam is going to handle what's coming, no matter what. It's going to be alright. "Just let me know if you need anything or if there's anything any of us can do to support you. I hope you feel like you can lean on us. I mean, anyone at HDH, we'll all help wherever we can, but especially me."

Tyler looks a little surprised, like maybe he was preparing himself for a more uncomfortable scene at drop-off. But no way. I'm not going to be that guy who piles on and adds even more stress onto his boyfriend's plate. Grown-Up Sam has this shit in hand. *Adulting FTW.*

We share a kiss before Tyler slides out of the truck and disappears through the sliding glass doors into the hospital. I just hope he knows how much I would do for him.

CHAPTER 27

TYLER

Sam drops me off at the main entrance to the hospital, and somehow, I manage to remember where to go, even though last night was such a fog. I feel a little weird. I think part of me thought Sam would fight me when I suggested he leave. But if he was here, it would just be one more thing I'd worry about. I know he would only want to help, but I'm so goddamn self-conscious about my family I'd never be able to think clearly, constantly wondering what he was thinking about all of us and our totally fucked-up dynamic.

But Sam is amazing. I want so badly to believe that he could end up being mine. And not just for a casual fuck or a friends-with-benefits situation. The part of me that wants Sam to be mine is growing out of control, and I don't know what to do with those feelings. But right now, I have other shit to deal with, so I put a pin in it for now.

There's a different nurse at the desk when I get to my mother's floor, and she gives me a warm smile. "I bet you're Tyler, right?" she says, surprising me.

"Um, yes."

"Tonya told me you'd be here early. The doctor hasn't been by yet. You can go sit with your mom if you want right now," she says in what I think is a Filipino accent.

"Um, okay, thank you," I say and make my way down to my mother's room.

My mother's roommates appear to be eating breakfast when I walk in, and I duck my head so they don't try to start conversation with me. I'm frankly not in the mood.

I take the chair beside my mom's bed, deciding I'd better make myself comfortable. It's warm in the room, so I take off my jacket and sweatshirt and go to tuck them into my backpack when I feel something I wasn't expecting. Confused, I pull out a paperback novel. It's an M/M romance Sam talked about when we were walking on the beach last week, which feels like a lifetime ago. He said it was one of the best books he's ever read. He must have stuck his copy into my backpack. Warmth spreads through my tummy like syrup. It's getting harder and harder to tell myself that there's no way Sam could ever want me. He keeps doing these sweet things and making these kind gestures that show me he thinks of me as more than just a fuck buddy. It's just so hard for me to believe someone so amazing thinks I'm special. But Sam sure seems to.

I spend the next couple of hours sitting by my mother's bed as she sleeps. She doesn't move, and if it wasn't for the steady pattern of the line on her heart monitor screen, I might be worried. Part of me wants her to wake up, and part of me really doesn't. I'm afraid of what she'll be like if she does wake up. If she remembers me, will she be as vile and awful as she was the last time I spoke to her? Or will she be pulling out the nice Dr. Jekyll version of herself and treat me with at least a tiny amount of respect? I guess I'll have to wait and see.

The doctor finally shows up just before lunchtime. He's an older man with kind but observant eyes, and I get the feeling he doesn't miss much.

"So, what questions do you have?" he asks after he checks the tablet attached to her bed. Good. I like the directness.

"I guess the biggest question is what is happening with her? How is she doing? What can we expect when she wakes up?"

He clears his throat and looks at me with level blue eyes. "I need to be honest with you, Tyler. The prognosis isn't great. The tumble down those stairs not only broke her ribs, but it also gave her a skull fracture. Because her health is so poor and we aren't able to get her up and moving around, I think she might be developing some fluid in her lungs, which we will try to manage and take care of before it turns into pneumonia, but I won't lie—if that happens, her chances of recovery go way down."

I let out a shaky sigh. "Do you... do you know what we can expect from her mentally after this? Will she be worse?"

He looks down at his files and reads for a moment before looking up at me. "No one can say for sure, Tyler, but if I were you, I would prepare myself for two possible outcomes. The first would be that we can get her physically stable and she's able to make a recovery. But, and this is just from experience, I suspect that her dementia will take another nosedive. After major incidents like this, patients often experience a decline, and given what happened before the accident and how she was already beginning to act out against other people, it's possible she may have been at the beginning of another disease-related decline. There's a good chance this will accelerate it."

I nod. The information isn't a surprise, but hearing it straight from the doctor is different.

"The other possible outcome is, quite simply, she doesn't wake up and succumbs to her injuries. I'm sorry to have to tell you that given the advanced nature of her disease and the seriousness of her injuries, I think it's more likely than the first outcome, honestly. But people often surprise me, so we never know what can happen."

I nod, letting that information wash over me, waiting to feel something. I'm not sure what I'm waiting for. Sorrow, anger, hatred. I don't know... Instead, there's... nothing. A doctor just told me there's a good chance my mother could die without even waking up, and I feel nothing. That can't be healthy, right?

"Okay." I clear my throat. "Thank you for being so honest. I. Um. I guess we just wait and see now?"

He nods. "For the most part, yes. Your mother has a do-not-resuscitate order on her file, so that means we will not take extraordinary measures to keep her alive, should it reach that point. I just need to make sure you're aware of that."

I nod. "That makes sense."

He gives me a kind smile as he gets up to leave, patting me gently on the shoulder as I sit numbly beside my mother's bed.

CHAPTER 28

TYLER

Late in the afternoon, I'm sitting beside my mother's bed, reading the paperback Sam left in my backpack this morning, when Aaron charges into the room like a man on a mission.

He stops when he sees me before breaking into a smile, but I know him well enough to see that it's forced. It's been more than two years since we've been face-to-face. We've texted and FaceTimed, but haven't actually been in the same room since shortly after our big argument. I admit, I usually tried to time my visits to my mother to when I knew he wouldn't be there. Cowardly, I know.

But now we're face-to-face again.

"Um, hey there," I say.

"Hi," he says, somewhat uneasily.

I get out of my chair, and we exchange an awkward bro-hug. It's clear neither of us has a clue how to handle this.

"So, um. Have you talked to the doctor?" He's talking unnaturally loudly. Clearly, he doesn't remember he no longer has to do that; between my hearing aids and the fact that I've gotten better at lip-reading, there's no need to yell. Not to mention the fact that I hate how yelling draws attention—not that the other people in this room will notice or care... but still...

"I look around and wave my hands in the air in a "cut it out" motion. "Shhh—Aaron, you don't have to yell. Hearing aids, remember?" I gesture toward my ears, fighting back the anger and sadness that wells up inside me at the fact that my brother doesn't know how to talk to me. At least he has the decency to look embarrassed.

"Ohh, shit, sorry. I... um, I forgot. It's, ah... been a while, I guess." He looks so sheepish that I start to feel kind of guilty myself. It's not like our estrangement is his fault alone.

"It's fine, don't worry about it. There's a lot going on," I say, forcing myself to let it go. Wasting energy on useless resentment toward

Aaron isn't going to help anyone. "But yeah, I spoke to the doctor earlier." I glance over at our mother, who hasn't moved the entire time I've been sitting here, which is now most of the day.

"Can we leave her here for a bit?" Aaron asks. "Maybe we should go get something to eat, and you can tell me what the doctor said? I came here straight from the airport, and I'm starving."

"Yeah, sure," I say. If she hasn't stirred all day, it's unlikely she's going to start now.

After I stop at the nurses' station to tell them where we're going, we head down to the cafeteria.

Once we have our meals, both of us settling on a bowl of tomato soup and a sandwich, we find a table in the corner, removed from the few other people scattered around.

"So, what have they told you so far?" Aaron asks once we're settled. "I talked to the people at Tall Firs, but it doesn't sound like they've exactly been keeping up with what the doctors are saying now. I think they're expecting you to do that."

I nod. "Yeah. So, the doctor isn't exactly optimistic." I relay what Dr. Nye told me earlier.

Once I'm finished, he shakes his head, staring down into his soup. He lets out a sigh and pushes the tray away, resting his elbows on the edge of the table. He holds his head in his hands for a moment before looking up at me.

"Fuck," he says. "Did anyone tell you how she ended up here in the first place?"

I nod. "The nurse told me there was some kind of altercation with another resident, but I don't have any details other than they both fell down the stairs."

He shakes his head. "Yeah. They told me she's been acting strangely toward this old guy who recently moved onto their floor. She alternates between getting viciously angry at him and coming onto him. And from what it sounds like, this guy isn't as far gone as she is, so he still remembers that he has a wife and wants nothing to do with her, which sets her off. Somehow, she cornered him at the top of the staircase and started trying to feel him up or something. When he turned her down, she got angry, so she shoved him. I guess he grabbed at her to try to stop from falling, but they both went down."

"Fuck," I mutter. "They told me the first night the other person wasn't hurt as bad though?"

"Yeah. She took the worst of the damage, thank god. He was brought to the hospital, but he only had a few bumps and bruises."

I nod. "Um, is there any chance they could try to sue her? Sue us, I guess, for what she did?"

Aaron blows out a breath. "I don't know. I'd need to check with a lawyer, but they've told the staff at the home they don't want to do that. As long as she gets moved to a ward where she's getting properly supervised, they'll be satisfied." He shakes his head. "It sounds like this guy and his family are actually more concerned that she gets proper care than they are about suing anyone." Aaron snorts. "Figures, right? This might be the one guy she's ever gone after who's not a complete and total dirtbag, and she ends up nearly killing him."

I bark out a laugh. "Yeah. Pretty typical."

"I would say so," Aaron says, shaking his head again. "I just... fuck. Thank god she qualified for social security and state insurance. I don't know what we'd do otherwise."

I nod, knowing full well how lucky we are in this state.

"So, I guess it's just a waiting game now?" I look down at the Formica tabletop, scratching idly at some years-old stain.

"Yeah, I guess it is."

Once we get back up to her room, we can see that Tonya or one of the other nurses has changed her bedding and her bandages. She looks almost peaceful lying there, but she seems so damn small. It's unnerving.

"So, you gave up your apartment, right? Do you want to stay at my place?" Aaron asks, sitting down in one of the chairs beside the bed.

I nod. "Yeah, as long as that's okay."

"Yeah, sure. I feel like I should stay here with her for a while since I haven't been here all day, but if she's just sleeping..." Aaron trails off, chewing his bottom lip, clearly trying to decide what to do. I'm sure he wants to go home after spending most of the day on a plane. Especially if the other option is staying here with our unconscious, shitty mother, who, if she does wake up, is more likely to hurl abuse at him than anything else. And, truthfully, if the roles were reversed, it's unlikely she would even bother showing up at the hospital at all.

"I think we should leave her. I've been here all day, and nothing's changed. I think it's fine for you to go home and rest, A." I put a hand on my brother's shoulder.

"Yeah, you're right. There's probably not much point in staying here. Let's head home."

CHAPTER 29

SAM

It takes me until I'm halfway back to Seattle to process the fact that Tyler basically sent me packing. Naturally, my first reaction is to freak out, replaying all our interactions, trying to figure out how I fucked it up. My normal internal monologue yells at me that I'm too boring and ordinary for someone like Tyler, but gradually, the voice of reason is beginning to overpower it, telling me to relax. I've given Tyler the space he asked for, and I didn't push him when he didn't want to talk about what was going on. He's going through a lot of shit; it makes sense he needs time to process it. Once he can get stuff with his family sorted, he'll have time for whatever this thing is between us. I know holding to him too tightly will only push him away. *Man alive, look at me being all adult and shit.*

"Hey, Siri, call Mason," I say to my phone, and a minute later, my cousin picks up.

"Hey, Sammy, how are things? How's Tyler?"

"Hey, Mase. Yeah, Tyler's okay. His brother got back into town today, and Ty's going to stay with him for a few days, so I thought I'd come home for the rest of the weekend."

There's the briefest pause before Mason responds. I haven't told him anything about what's happened between Tyler and me over the last few weeks, but I have an inkling he knows more than he's letting on right now. It's fine with me if he's figured it out. I'm not going to keep secrets from him anymore. It's time to come clean about everything.

"That makes sense. Where are you now? You've got your condo rented out, right? You want to stay in the guest house for the weekend?" he asks. I'd been able to sublet my amazing condo for the next few months to a friend of Jax's from LA. He's an NHL hockey player who was recently traded to the Seattle team. He was sick of staying in a hotel but didn't want to get into a long-term lease, so my condo was the perfect solution for both of us.

"Yeah, that'd be good. I was kind of hoping to get together with everyone for drinks or dinner. Do you know if everyone's free?"

He chuckles. "Yeah, stay with us. And are you officially requesting a meeting of the Council of Cousins? You know we'll all make time for something so important." I can hear the smile in his voice. The four of us will always make time for each other.

"No one was expecting me, so if you guys have plans, I don't want—"

"Dude," Mason interrupts, "we're all middle-aged, married, and boring. I'm pretty sure your coming into town will be the highlight of all of our weekends. Do you want to get together with just the four of us, or will it work if the other halves are hanging around? Jax and I can host everyone tomorrow for dinner."

"Yeah, that sounds great, man, thanks. I'm cool with having everyone there. I'm going to pop into Mom and Dad's place today, but I'll sleep at the guest house tonight. If I don't catch you then, I'll head over in the morning."

I hang up with Mason and spend the last part of my drive home wondering how much I should tell everyone tomorrow. I'm desperate for some advice on how to deal with what's going on between Tyler and me. I want to tell them about my job offer in California. It's probably a discussion I should have with Mason and Dylan privately first, although it's not like Grace and all the partners don't know everything that happens around the office anyway. I'll have to play it by ear. The last thing I want to do is hurt anyone, least of all Mason.

After spending the afternoon at my parents' house, I head over to Mason and Jackson's guesthouse to sleep. It feels weird to be here since the last time I was here was the night of the storm when Tyler and I hooked up... How was that only a few weeks ago?

Every time my phone makes a sound, I jump, hoping like hell it's Tyler, but so far, I've heard nothing. But hanging out with my parents for the afternoon brought home the reality of how different Tyler's life was growing up. It makes me so sad that he doesn't have anyone in his life to support him the way my parents and my extended family do for me. If he lets me, I'll be that person for him, and my family will become his.

On Sunday afternoon, after a lazy morning in bed by myself, I walk up to the main house, and after a couple of quick raps, I let myself in, announcing my presence with a yodel. Two seconds later, Harry and Sally, their pair of Labrador retrievers, come bounding down the hallway toward me, and I get down on my knees to give them both some love. One of these days, I'll break down and get a dog of my own, but up until now, I've resisted.

But after all the thinking I've been doing, I'm starting to wonder why that is. Have I really been putting off getting a dog because I'm too busy and not home enough? Or has it just been another thing I've been pushing off to the side, part of me that I'm keeping buried in case some random person comes along who I think I'm in love with, and I want to keep myself open and available to mold into whatever I think they want me to be? I shake my head again, and then I'm pulled back out of my daydream as Harry slurps a giant, wet kiss right on my mouth.

"Ugh, gross!" I shout at him, shoving him gently away from me and scrambling to my feet. "I love you, buddy, but not that way! Blech!" I'm wiping my mouth on the back of my sleeve and toeing off my shoes at the same time when I hear a chuckle. Mason's standing at the far end of the hallway, laughing at me.

"Don't deny it. You love Harry's kisses." He grins at me. "I would normally make a crack about how that's the most action you've seen in a while, but something tells me that might not be the case these days, hmmm?" He cocks an eyebrow at me as we head into the kitchen, where Jackson is standing over the big chef-grade gas cooktop, stirring something that smells like heaven.

"Sammy!" Jax's face lights up when he sees me, coming over to wrap me in a big hug. He's not as tall or as built as Mason is, but he's still bigger than I am, and there's something about Jackson Cullen that simply makes people comfortable. He's been that way since the minute we met him. No pretense at all, even though he's a huge movie star. Mason picked himself a good one.

"Everyone else will be here soon," Mason says, handing me a beer. "We got lucky—even Reed is off tonight, so it'll be the full quorum at the Council of Cousins." He smiles, taking a sip from his own beer. Reed works in the ER so much it can be hard to find a night he's not working. "I'm glad you're here a little early though. I want to find out what's going on with Tyler."

I blow out a breath as we both get comfortable on the barstools that line the massive kitchen island across from where Jax is working on dinner.

"Well, I haven't heard from him since I left Tacoma yesterday. He didn't share much with me, but it doesn't seem like things are going well. He was upset and didn't want to talk about it after he talked to the doctor on Friday night." I hold back from sharing what he did want to do that evening. Some things are best kept private.

"That sucks." Mason shakes his head, and Jackson's face is a mask of sympathy.

"It really is," I say. "Apparently, his mom was a severe alcoholic for most of her life, and her dementia is made worse by the fact that she was such a heavy drinker. It's fucking sad. Sometimes it's easy to forget how lucky we are with our family." I look at Mason, who reaches over and places a hand gently over Jackson's where it's resting on the island. The two of them share a small smile.

"So, is Tyler okay? I'm kind of surprised you didn't stay down there with him," Mason says, one eyebrow cocked, and I know he knows something's up.

"Yeah," I say. "I'm surprised too." I blow out a sigh, trying to figure out where to start while Mason and Jax wait patiently.

"You don't need to go over everything since you're going to have to repeat yourself when everyone gets here. Just give me the relevant bits for work—like is whatever's going on with you two going to affect work? Is this something serious, or are you friends with benefits? What are you thinking here?"

"I think it could be serious. But you know me, I always think things could be serious." I roll my eyes.

Jackson tries unsuccessfully to stifle a giggle, and Mason snorts a laugh, not even trying to hide it. "True story, cousin. But I'm sensing you're feeling something different with Tyler?"

I sometimes think Mason missed his true calling. He would have made a great shrink. Or, even better, a psychic. It's like the man can read minds.

I think about his question. "Yeah, I do feel different this time. I feel calmer. Less worried about whether things will work out. I mean, I'm really into him, and I think he's into me. But I'm not losing my mind over it." I shake my head. "The reason I'm here is because he said he needed to deal with things together with his brother. He needed some space. Normally, I'd be freaking the fuck out. But I've been pretty calm. I'm just kind of trusting he'll call me when he's ready." I shrug, taking a swig from my beer.

"Ohhh, how sweet. Our little Sammy is growing up and adulting now!" Mason teases, and I shoot him a dirty look.

"But whether it's going to affect work... well, I need to talk to you and Dyl about that."

"Wait, what does that mean?" There's a note of concern in Mason's voice. I take a deep breath and square my shoulders. *Just rip the Band-Aid off.* "Okay, look. I should have probably told you guys about this a while ago, and I should probably wait until Dylan gets here to tell you... but I was offered a job somewhere else. In Southern California, to be exact."

"Wait—what?" Mason's shocked expression matches Jackson's as both of their mouths hang open. "And you're thinking about taking it?" he asks, wide-eyed.

I bite my lip and nod, hating the hurt look on Mason's face. But I have to do this, for me. "Yeah. I kind of am." I pick nervously at the label of my beer bottle, desperate for something to do with my hands. "Do you remember Shane? From my landscape architecture classes?"

"Yeah, of course. You guys hung out a lot," Mason says, his brows knitted in confusion.

"He called me a few weeks ago. He started a landscape and pool design business in Southern California. He's already got more clients than he can manage, and he asked me to move down and partner with him."

There's a stunned silence as Mason looks at me, his mouth hanging open.

"I would never have thought I'd be interested, you know, Mase, but I don't know, I think when you bought in and you and Dyl became full partners in HDH, I started feeling like maybe I was falling behind. And, I mean, things have gotten a little weird between you and me, and I don't know if it's because now I technically work for you or what, but it's weird, and I don't want whatever is going on to change us. You're more than a cousin; you're my brother, and, fuck, things just haven't been feeling right...?" I can hear myself babbling, but I'm not sure how to stop. I hate this. I don't want to hurt my cousins. By the time I stop running my mouth, my eyes are burning with unshed tears. I don't feel much better when Mason finally closes his mouth, his lips narrowing into a thin line.

"I'm sorry, Mase. I really am. I just—"

He holds up a hand to stop me before I start rambling again. "It's fine. Let's just table this discussion until Dylan gets here because he needs to be part of this. I just need to know if you've accepted this job in California yet? Are we going to have to plan around you leaving?"

I shake my head furiously. "No, of course not. I've asked Shane to give me a few more weeks. I was planning on giving him an answer earlier, but with everything going on with this new project, I know I can't just walk away at the drop of a hat." I pause, taking a long swig from my beer. "He gets it, but he needs an answer from me soon since he needs to find someone else to partner with if I say no. But now, to make all this shit even more complicated, there's this... this... whatever this thing is between me and Tyler. I'm so fucking confused. And I'm sorry if this hurts your feelings, Mase. I don't want to—"

"Sammy, it's okay." Mason gives me a reassuring smile and reaches out to give my arm a squeeze. "I'm just surprised. I guess I didn't know you were feeling that way... but you're right, we haven't been as connected lately—between the growing business and... stuff... with me and Jax... I guess I missed it. I'm sorry, man. But we'll get it sorted out tonight."

Just as he finishes, the front door opens, ushering in the noise and commotion that comes along with the rest of our family. Sure enough, a minute later, a small pack of dogs comes racing around the corner, Mason and Jackson's dogs, Harry and Sally, in the lead, followed closely by David, Alexis, and Kramer, Dylan and Reed's three dogs. It appears Grace and Derek didn't include their dogs in the mix today, probably because their hands are full enough with their toddler, Kellan.

The cacophony of this loud clan of Campbells is like a peanut butter and jelly sandwich—simple, familiar, and so comforting to me. I can't imagine living my life without this ridiculous crew of crazies in it.

The next hour or so is taken up with all the shouty, yelly, funny laughter and teasing we always go through when we haven't seen each other for a while. This group is undoubtedly insane, but they're my insane crew, and being with them is like snuggling into a cozy blanket.

After the madness has run its course, and the dogs have been fed, and toddler Kellan is ensconced in his high chair, happily shoving Cheerios in his mouth, Jax and Mason bring out the food, and we all gather around the table.

CHAPTER 30

SAM

The madness continues for a while, and I soak it all in. *Could I really leave these people I love so much?* As we're finishing, Mason clears his throat.

"Okay, crazies. Sammy here asked for a get-together with all of us, and based on the conversation we had right before you all walked in, there's a lot we need to talk about. I know we're all curious about whatever the fuck is going on with you and Tyler"—Mason glances at me—"but you mentioned some stuff right before dinner that we need to deal with before getting to the good stuff." He grins, while Grace takes the opportunity to get up and wipe off Kellan's grubby little hands and face before pulling him out of his high chair and setting him on the floor to play with his toys.

"Okay, Sammy, why don't you share with the class?" Mason says.

"Okay." I take a deep breath. "Well, as I told Mason before dinner, nothing has actually happened with this yet, it's just... A few weeks ago, I got a call from an old friend. He's got his own landscape architecture business down in Orange County, in California, and he wants me to move down there and partner with him."

There's a stunned silence around the table while everyone takes this in. I assume Mason was able to pull Dylan aside and let him know what was happening, but it looks like everyone else is stunned.

"Wait," Gracie says. "You're not actually considering this, are you? You're not seriously thinking about moving to California?"

I clear my throat uncomfortably and look down at my plate, which contains the remains of Jackson's delicious lasagna and Caesar salad. "Well... I... I haven't given him an answer yet," I say, speaking into my plate. It's easier than looking at Grace. "But it's a really great opportunity."

"You're considering this? For real?" Grace asks, her tone rising. She looks at Mason, a weird combination of anger and amusement on her face.

"Well, assholes, are you going to tell him or what?" she says bluntly. Mason barks out a laugh, while Derek, Jackson, and Reed all look like cats who ate a bunch of canaries.

"Tell me what, exactly?" I ask.

Mason gives me a sheepish look and trades glances with Dylan. "We really should have told you this a while ago, Sam. I'm so sorry we didn't—especially since you've been feeling weird about the dynamics around here for a while. I feel like an asshole. But we need to tell you something."

"What?" I have literally no idea what they're talking about.

Dylan takes over the conversation. "Sam, we've been working on a few things, and we definitely should have told you sooner what we're thinking about. But we want to expand the business into Oregon, and we were thinking you could take over that branch. You could buy in, and we'd all be equal partners."

"Wait, what?" It's my turn to be stunned. "You want me to buy in, now? How... How long has this been going on?" I stammer, feeling like my world has just tipped on its axis. I'm seeing everything differently than I was only a few minutes ago.

Dylan gets the same sheepish look on his face that Mason has, which means he really must feel terrible because he doesn't usually wear his emotions on his sleeve.

"We started talking about it a few months ago. We've already talked to the bank and everything."

"Wait, this has been in the works for months and you didn't think to tell me?" I ask, feeling equally annoyed and thrilled.

"I'm so sorry we didn't. It's mostly my fault," Mason interjects. "I got distracted with personal stuff in the last few weeks, and this got put onto the back burner. The stupid thing is that after I talked to you yesterday, we talked and decided to tell you tonight. We even told Gracie and Derek so they could stop and get one of those amazing cream puff cakes from that bakery you love to celebrate. I mean, if you want to accept our offer. You don't have to. I mean, if the California thing is what you really want to do..." His voice trails off.

"We owe you a huge apology," Dylan says calmly. "We should have known the imbalance in the power structure might be weird, and we should have dealt with it sooner. I'm really sorry."

"Fuck, I got my head stuck up my own ass, and I'm so fucking sorry about it, man. I really hope we haven't fucked this whole thing up and lost you to another job because we were being idiots and took you for granted," Mason says. His voice sounds a little wobbly, like he's really emotional.

"Holy shit," I say softly. "Well, that's great. I mean, thanks, guys. I just... I'm not sure exactly how to handle all this right now. I mean, I always planned to stay in this part of the world, you all know that, it's just... there's a lot of other shit to think about now too." My head is still spinning from everything I've learned in the last five minutes.

"Sam, I don't want you to stress about it," Mason says. "We obviously want you to stay, but more than anything, we want you to be happy. If that means going to California, we'll all be sad, but we'll deal with it."

I nod, and the uncertainty in Mason's voice is surprising, but there's a little part of me that likes it. I'm glad he knows now that he really can't take me for granted.

"We also want you to be sure of whatever you decide," Dylan says, and I look at him. He usually doesn't speak much at these gatherings unless he's asked directly about something. But he's clearly feeling strongly. "But we'll support you with whatever you decide to do," he says.

"Okay, why don't we change the topic for now and let Sam digest all that for a bit," Mason says, directing a smile at me.

"Yeah. Right now, we need to know what's happening between you and that sweet little thang named Tyler..." Grace giggles.

I roll my eyes, and strangely, the stuff with Tyler doesn't seem quite as hard to talk about. I didn't realize keeping my job offer a secret was weighing on me so heavily. I feel so much lighter.

"So, yeah... Well. Tyler and I are kind of a thing. At least, I think we are..."

I look at Grace, who's busy making the "speed it up" signal with her hand.

"Yeah, yeah, we know you're a thing. You two have only been making eyes at each other for about three years now." She smiles. "What's happening now that you're out there on the coast together, hidden away at a romantic beach resort, snuggled up inside as the storms rage outside?" Grace gets a dreamy look on her face.

I look over at Mason. "Did you happen to tell them about our accommodations?"

Jax snorts into his beer.

"Ah, no, I haven't gotten to that. You should definitely tell us all about your ocean-side love shack out there."

Grace lifts an eyebrow, and I proceed to fill them in on what's been going on between Tyler and me for the past few weeks.

I must gush on about him for waaaay too long because when I finally stop talking, there are several bemused expressions staring back at me.

"What?" I ask, a little defensive. Everyone laughs, but Jax is the one who holds up a glass in a mock toast. "Mate... you luuuuurrrve him..."

Everyone cracks up, and I roll my eyes. "I don't know... I... It's way too early to think about that. And besides, I haven't even gotten to the part where he told me to take a hike."

"What do you mean he told you to take a hike?" Grace asks. Kellan starts to fuss on the floor, and Derek gets up to take care of him.

Also, I suspect, to try not to overhear too much of the conversation in case Tyler wants to talk about it in therapy.

I let out a sigh, coming back to Earth with a thunk after rhapsodizing about how amazing Tyler is for the last few minutes.

"So, Tyler's mom is in a care home, and he got a call on Friday afternoon telling him she'd fallen down the stairs and was in the hospital, and he needed to get there quickly. I drove him in to Tacoma. He went in to visit her that night, but, but she was unconscious, and there wasn't anyone around who could give him much detail about her condition. He was pretty upset and overwhelmed after seeing her, so I'm guessing things aren't looking great. I offered to stay with him, but he said he was more comfortable handling it with his brother. He needed some space, so I'm trying to give it to him. You know. Like an adult." I can't resist sassing them all a little bit.

"Wow, poor Tyler. Sounds like he's got a lot on his plate. I think you did the right thing by giving him space if he asked for it. Very adult-y of you, Sam. Congratulations." Grace grins at me and raises her wineglass in a toast.

"I don't know him very well, but I think giving him space to deal with his family crap is a good idea too," Reed says thoughtfully. "But maybe remind him every so often that you're ready when he does want to talk. Speaking as someone who comes from a shit upbringing, there's a ton of shame around it, even though there shouldn't be, so it's good not to press him." Dylan is looking at Reed with a fond smile on his face. Dyl isn't the touchy-feely type, but it's obvious how much he loves Reed. It hits me in the chest. I want that. I really fucking want that.

"It can be hard to adjust to having someone care about you if you haven't had it. I agree with Reed—let him know you're there if or when he wants to talk. He seems like a great guy. He'll get himself sorted," Jackson says.

I nod, absorbing the advice. "I can do that. I think. But this shit is more complicated than it should be." Everyone laughs.

"Always is," Mason chuckles.

I'm about to push back from the table since an early night sounds like a good idea when Mason clears his throat again.

"Anyway, before we break up this little party, Jax and I have one more piece of news you all might be interested in." His eyes are twinkling, and Jax looks like he's ready to bust out of his skin with excitement.

We all hold our breaths for a moment while Mason lets the suspense build, and just as I think Grace is about to lose her mind, he shouts, "We're having a baby!"

The room erupts in cheers and laughter as everyone jumps up to congratulate Mason and Jax on their amazing news. We've all been expecting it for a while, and again, I'm hit in the gut with a weird happy and sad feeling. Turns out that not only do I want a relationship like theirs, but apparently, I still want to do the whole family thing. I want it all. I had tried to put that desire out of my mind for a long time, again wanting to keep all my options open for when the mythical "Mr. or Miss Right" came along. I wanted to be able to twist myself into exactly who I thought they'd want. But it's becoming more and more clear to me that isn't the best way to go about things.

Mason breaks out the champagne as he explains that the surrogate they were matched with a few months back is apparently a real fertile Myrtle, and she got pregnant on their first round of IVF. It's still early, but the two of them are walking on air, and as envious as I am, it's amazing to see them so happy. Mason and Jax are going to make incredible parents, and no matter what happens with Tyler and me, I'll be there as the trusty uncle.

CHAPTER 31

TYLER

After leaving the hospital, we go to Aaron's condo. He's moved since we saw each other last. His new place is small and old, but it's clean and in a much better part of town than I was living in. He shows me to the tiny extra room with an old pull-out couch in it and goes to shower. We decide to order takeout and watch some Netflix before going to bed early. We need to figure out some kind of schedule for being at the hospital for the next few days, at least until Mom's condition is stable, but we don't have to figure that out this minute. More importantly, Aaron and I have stuff to discuss.

The pizza arrives, and we take it to his living room, each grabbing a slice. Aaron goes to grab the remote to turn on the TV, but I stop him.

I swallow my nerves and bite the bullet. "Wait, Aaron, we should talk about some stuff."

He heaves a sigh and looks back at me. "Yeah, you're probably right." He stares down at his plate. "I've been like an ostrich with my head in the sand." He snorts. "I'm just not great with this kind of shit."

I snort back at him. "And somehow you think I am?" I scoff. "We were raised by the same person, Aar. It's a fucking wonder either of us can do anything more than grunt and point at shit to communicate."

"Ha. That'd be a lot easier."

I chuckle. "So anyway, I just got a raise at work, and I want to contribute more to paying off her debt."

My brother shakes his head and pushes his chair back from the table, evidently uncomfortable with the conversation. "It's fine, Ty. Don't worry about it. Whatever you can contribute is great. I'm managing."

I fucking hate that he feels like the entire burden of Mom's debt and managing her care and everything else falls on his shoulders alone.

Especially since it was him she stole from, his life forever changed because of her thoughtless choices and selfishness. Aaron had been close to a major break in his career when he had to rush home and deal with her while I was overseas. He'd been asked to work with Cody West, one of the hottest, up-and-coming country stars around, and he was through the roof with excitement. On the FaceTime chats we used to have before my accident, he'd been so happy and positive about the future. But when he started getting calls from Social Services about Mom, he put everything on hold, including his work with Cody, to come home and tend to her. He worked so hard to drag himself out of the gutter we started out in, only for our mother to once again drag him down as he got close to the top. If Mom hadn't burdened him with this financial mess or ruined his credit score, he wouldn't have to work a million hours and could devote more time to music.

"Aaron, I'm serious. I really want to help more. I want you to be able to spend more time on your songwriting. Plus, you need to be in Nashville more often. I can deal with the stuff with Mom once we get through this crisis."

He bites his lip and looks at me. "Okay, Ty. Thank you. Whatever you can do, I appreciate it."

I nod, glad he didn't fight me too hard. Aaron's not finished though.

"Tyler, I'm, uh—I just want you to know I'm sorry for what I said when we... last talked... I said a lot of awful shit, and I didn't mean it. I knew it wasn't true. I was just... I wanted to hurt you the same way I felt like I was getting hurt, you know? I was overwhelmed and fucked-up, and the easiest thing was to blame you instead of facing what was happening."

Well, this is unexpected.

"Ummm..." I say, and Aaron looks at me, pushes away from the table, and starts pacing around the living room, rubbing the back of his neck.

"I never should have said those things to you. Even as I was saying it, I knew it wasn't true. I knew you were never going to end up using me like Mom. You came home without your hearing, and all I could think of was how it was going to affect me. I didn't show you one ounce of compassion, and I'm so sorry. And then I was just too goddamn stubborn to man up and apologize, and now it's been years, and I'm an idiot."

I did not see this coming. I had hoped, and maybe even expected, that we'd be able to get past our argument. But his apology seems so sincere it's taking me off guard, and a lump rises in my throat. I can't let Aaron take all the blame for what happened.

"Aar, it's not all your fault. I was an asshole. I know I was. I mean, yeah, I was struggling with my own shit, but I shouldn't have just expected you to manage everything with her. That wasn't fair. I'm really sorry too."

We stare at each other for a second before Aaron steps closer and throws his arms around me. And suddenly, we're both fucking crying.

"Fuck, I'm sorry, Ty," he says, and I can feel his voice shake more than I can hear it. "I miss you so much."

"I'm sorry too, Aar. I miss you too, and I promise, I'm going to do better. We'll take care of this shit with Mom together."

After we break apart, both a little embarrassed from our outbursts, we clean up the kitchen together and then crash on the couch. We spend the rest of the evening in silence, but it's the good kind, the comfortable kind. I know that whatever needs to be resolved between us will be. We'll work it out because we love each other, and we need each other. Between Sam and now Aaron, for the first time in as long as I can remember, I feel like I'm not alone in this world, and a tiny spark of hope flickers to life inside me. Maybe, just maybe, things are turning around for me.

CHAPTER 32

TYLER

When I wake up, Aaron's in the kitchen, making us breakfast. Later today, we're meeting with Mom's care home to talk about what happens when she's well enough to return there.

It's still early when we get to her room. Early enough that the nurses haven't been in to wake everyone yet. Aaron says it's because he's on Tennessee time after his latest trip, so his clock is still a couple of hours ahead, but I think he feels obligated to be here.

"I'll go get us some coffee," I say and head down to the cafeteria. I remember how Aaron likes his coffee, same as mine, more cream and sugar than should be legal, and when I get back up to our room, the nurse has been in to open the blinds, letting light stream in through the window. It's a rare sunny winter day, and though it's still wet and cold, there's something springlike in the air.

I take the seat across the bed from Aaron, and we both settle in, sipping our coffees. Again, the silence between us isn't strained; it's comfortable, and I'm so happy to have my brother back.

We haven't been sitting there long when I catch movement out of the corner of my eye. Mom is moving one of her hands, her eyelids fluttering.

"Oh, fuck, Aar," I hiss. He looks at me and then over to her, his eyes widening when he realizes what's happening.

"Should we call someone?" I ask, but before Aaron can answer, she opens her eyes.

She blinks up at us a couple of times before the fog seems to clear. "Hi, boys," she says in a voice too soft for my hearing aids to pick up, but I read her lips. She smiles at us, and I can't tell if she knows what's happening or if she's locked in some memory of the past. It would have to be one of the rare decent memories because it wasn't often she gave us that soft, genuine smile and used a gentle voice with us.

"Um. Hi, Mom," Aaron says as he shoots me a sideways glance.

Our mother was always unpredictable, but since her dementia took over, it's impossible to tell what version of her we'll be seeing when she opens her mouth.

"Do you two remember that time we went to the County Fair and you both got cotton candy?" she says.

Aaron and I trade glances. "Yeah, Mom. We both remember that," he says. It's one of the rare good days we had together, one of the tiny handful of my happy memories of us. We had gone to the Washington State Fair—I must have been six or seven, and Aaron was a teenager. She bought us cotton candy, and I was completely covered in the stuff, my fingers and my face all blue from the food dye. Then we went on the roller coaster together, and the three of us just screamed with laughter. I'd been terrified and exhilarated all at once from the ride and the sugar but also from the excitement of having a good day with my mother. I was already old enough to recognize that the good days were few and far between.

She gets this dreamy smile on her face. "You two are both so handsome."

Aaron's eyes widen as he stares at me, and I'm probably reflecting that same expression right back at him.

"I'm sorry, boys," she says, and we both look at her, shocked. That may be the only time those words have come out of her mouth, and even though I'm not sure she even knows what she's apologizing for, it settles something inside me.

She closes her eyes and stays quiet for a moment before she reaches her un-casted hand toward us, so Aaron takes it, and I tentatively hold her fingers that are poking out the end of her casted arm. "You're good boys. You won't make my same mistakes." It almost seems like she's talking to herself until she opens her eyes again and looks at each one of us. "I love you," she says before squeezing Aaron's hand and curling her fingers around mine.

"I love you too, Mom," I say. She hasn't said those words to me since I was a child, and my eyes fill with tears, threatening to spill over. I look over to see Aaron struggling in a similar fashion.

"I love you, Mom," he says, and she gets a serene look on her face before she lets her head fall back against the pillow and closes her eyes, her muscles going slack as she drifts off again.

We're silent for a moment before Aaron straightens up, setting her hand down gently beside her and clearing his throat. It's like we both sense something important just happened, but we don't know what to do or how to handle it.

"We should probably tell someone she was awake, I guess?" I say, and he nods before pressing the call button.

When a nurse comes in a few minutes later, we tell her what happened, and she quickly takes my mother's vital signs. "Everything looks okay, so I'll call Dr. Nye and let him know she was awake," she says before heading out the door.

Aaron and I are left staring at each other, neither of us sure what to do now.

"I don't even know..." He trails off and looks back down at Mom, shaking his head.

"Me neither," I say.

Aaron and I sit together, mostly silent, until the doctor comes in about half an hour later. After we tell him what happened, he looks thoughtful for a moment and then grabs a chair, which he pulls up to the foot of Mom's bed. Then he pulls the curtain around us for a little privacy.

"So, this sounds like something I've seen a few times. I can't say for sure, but it sometimes happens when people are coming close to the end of their lives. They call it paradoxical lucidity or terminal lucidity. It's when someone who has been experiencing dementia for a long time suddenly returns to mental clarity. It's like they come back from wherever they've gone. We don't understand it yet, so I can't tell you what it means in your mother's case. She could wake up and have another lucid, clear moment, and you'll be able to talk to her as if she was never sick. Or she could wake up and be just as confused as before or potentially worse. We just don't know." His smile is kind. "I'm sorry I can't give you anything more."

After the doctor leaves, Aaron and I are sort of at a loss for what we should do. Neither one of us brings up Mom's episode. I don't think either one of us knows what to make of it.

The rest of the day drags by, and she doesn't wake up again. It's after dinner when Aaron and I decide to head back to his place.

We get home and eat pad Thai out of little cardboard containers and still don't talk about what our mom said to us.

"So, are you dating anyone?" Aaron asks.

"Well, it's kind of... not really official yet... but yeah. I just started seeing someone in the last few weeks," I say.

"Yeah?" he says, a smile in his voice. "That guy you've been working with? The one who drove you here?"

I nod. "Yeah. He's amazing, Aar. He's older, but we're just... I like how he makes me feel, you know?"

Aaron looks at me with a level gaze when I'm done waxing poetic about Sam. "He sounds pretty special."

"He really is, but I don't know. I don't want to get too attached, you know? I don't want to get to the point where I'm depending on him."

Aaron looks confused for a second. "Depending on him for what? Money?"

"Well, not really. I don't need his money. It's just... everything else, I guess... I mean, I don't want to be fucked when he leaves."

Aaron shrugs. "I'm no expert, Ty... believe me. But from what you've told me, he sounds like a pretty good guy. And depending on him doesn't necessarily mean you're *dependent* on him. We don't have to make the same mistakes she did—becoming unable to function on her own. You can obviously take care of yourself, you've proven that over and over. But letting someone be there for you, letting them help you, support you, doesn't mean you're dependent on them. I mean, you'd want to do the same for him, right?"

I nod, letting his words sink in.

"It sounds like he's important to you, Ty. Don't let your fear of becoming like her stop you from trusting someone enough to let them support you."

"Yeah," I say as I process what he said. He's right. My reluctance to allow Sam to help me probably does come from fear of being like my mother. And there's no way I want to deny myself any more happiness because of something she did. I'm done living that way.

"So, what about you? Are you seeing anyone?"

A strange look passes over his face for a second, but it disappears quickly. "Nah. I was seeing a girl for a while. But I'm not anymore." His scowl indicates the subject is closed, and I sense that I shouldn't push him. Maybe someday we'll be able to get that close relationship back, but right now, I'm happy to have this much.

We're almost done with our third episode of some mindless reality show when Aaron's phone vibrates on the coffee table.

He glances at the screen and then looks at me as he swipes to answer it. "It's the hospital," he mouths.

His conversation is short. And I know. He doesn't even have to tell me when he hangs up. He just looks at me for a second.

"She's gone, isn't she?" I ask, and he nods.

"Yeah. She's gone."

CHAPTER 33

SAM

After our family dinner and Council of Cousins meeting wraps up, I head back to the guesthouse, feeling pretty good about things. I was sitting there with the family, surrounded by the craziness and love that I'm so fortunate to have in my life, and I know for sure that I don't want to leave. The opportunity in California is a great one, but the chance to grow what has become our family business is what I've been waiting for. I'm excited, and I can't wait to get planning for what the Oregon office of HDH will look like. I call my buddy Shane when I get up to the suite and let him know I've decided to stay where I am. He laughs when I tell him my decision.

"Honestly, man, I was fucking shocked when you said you'd consider it. I never thought you'd ever leave the PNW. I'm glad you gave it some thought, but it sounds like a great gig for you."

"Yeah, it is. I'm really excited. But thanks so much for thinking of me, and I'd love to come down at some point to check out the work you guys are doing down there."

We end the conversation, and I feel even better; like things might be settling into place for me. I want to talk to Tyler, but I don't have that sick feeling of desperation I normally get when I'm in a relationship. It's weird because normally, if I'd gone this long without contact from someone I was dating, I'd be beside myself. But things with Tyler are different. It's not because I care less, but because deep down inside, I just know it's going to work out the way it's supposed to. No matter what happens, we're going to be okay. Don't ask me why. I'm not going to question it, but the feeling is strong.

I've just crawled into bed when my phone dings. Grabbing it off the bedside table, I smile in the dark when I see Tyler's name pop up.

Tyler: You awake?

Me: Yup. Just getting into bed. How are you? How are things going?

Tyler: I'm okay. But my mom passed away today.

Oh shit. I sit straight up in bed, wishing I could hear his voice.

Me: Oh my god, I'm so sorry Tyler. Do you need me to come now?

Tyler: Sam, I'm okay, really. I want to see you, but let's wait until morning. Things with Aaron are going well, and I want one more night to hang out with just him.

I take a deep breath. Everything in my gut is pushing me to go see him right now, but I can hear the advice of my family. I need to make sure he knows I care and I'm here for him, but

I won't overdo it. He wants to spend this time with his brother. I need to respect that.

> *Me: Okay, no problem, I get it. But will you call me if you need anything? Any time?*

> *Tyler: I promise. Text me when you know what time you'll be here tomorrow.*

> *Me: It will be early.*

> *Tyler: lol. I know. I can't wait to see you.*

· · ● · ● · ● · ·

By the time the sun's coming up, I'm getting into the truck, heading down to see Tyler. It took all my determination to not get out of bed in the middle of the night and race down to be with him, but I didn't, and I know I'm doing the right thing. I know I can be what Tyler needs because that's just who I am. I don't need to change. I don't need to contort myself into all these different shapes, trying to be what I think someone's looking for. Tyler needs me to be myself. I wasn't trying to be someone else when we met, and I haven't tried since. We're right for each other exactly as we are. I'm not sure if Tyler has figured it out yet, but he will. I just know.

An hour later, I pull up to the address Tyler gave me for his brother's place, a condo in what looks like a decent part of town.

Leaving all my stuff in the car since I'm not entirely sure where I'll be staying tonight, I buzz the apartment number, and a voice I don't recognize comes over the intercom.

"Hi, Sam. Come on up." I guess it must be Aaron. He sounds friendly enough, although I'll reserve judgement until I see how he treats Tyler.

The door of the condo opens as I'm stepping off the elevator a few moments later, and Tyler comes out of the apartment. He's wearing jeans and a tight black T-shirt that clings to his lean body and makes my mouth water. His tattoos are peeking out from under his sleeve, and he looks amazing. He jogs down the hall toward me and, without hesitation, throws his arms around my neck, capturing my mouth with his.

"Oof," I mumble into his mouth, but then I respond eagerly. God, he feels so good in my arms. Like he belongs there.

"Hi," I say with a smile when we finally break apart.

He's giving off a different vibe. He seems more open, more unguarded or something. I could be projecting, but maybe I'm not the only one who worked through some feelings over the past few days.

"Hi," he says, and we stare into each other's eyes for a moment before he kisses me again and unwraps himself from around me. "Come on in and meet Aaron." He leads me into the condo, where I find a slightly taller, bulkier version of Tyler. They look so much alike, with the same short, dark hair, bright blue eyes, and smattering of freckles across his nose and cheeks, making him look way younger than I know he is. He's got a jacket on and looks like he's heading out somewhere.

"Aaron, hi. It's nice to meet you," I say, extending my hand.

"Nice to meet you too, Sam," he answers. For a beat, I feel like we're two dogs sniffing each other's butts, trying to determine if we're friends or enemies.

"I'm so sorry to hear about your mother," I say to both of them. I'm not sure what Tyler needs from me yet, whether he wants me to be actively helping him get things done or if he wants me to just be here to loan him some strength. Whatever he needs, I can do it.

"Thanks," both brothers say at the same time.

"Come on in. Are you hungry or anything? Thirsty? We finally ordered groceries, so there's actually some food here," Tyler says, leading me into the kitchen.

"I'm okay. I'll just have a glass of water." I take a seat at one of the barstools by the kitchen counter.

"Hey, guys, I'm just going to head out for a little while. Got something to take care of. It was nice meeting you, Sam," Aaron says, giving us a quick wave before heading out the door.

"So, tell me. How are you doing?" I ask as Tyler places my water in front of me and settles onto the barstool beside me.

He smiles, and there's something different about it. He looks... lighter almost.

He grabs one of my hands. "I'm good, Sam. I'm really, really good, for the first time in a long time."

And he fills me in on what's happened the last couple of days.

"Wow," I say when he's finished. "How do you feel about everything?"

"I've been thinking about it nonstop, and I've made a couple of decisions," he says.

I raise an eyebrow at him. "Yeah?"

He stands up and steps closer to me, and I move so he's standing between my legs, his hands on my shoulders.

"I've spent my whole life trying to make sure I never had to depend on anyone for anything because I was so afraid of becoming like her. Just jumping from guy to guy, always relying on someone else to take care of her problems, The nicer guys just got tired of it and left her, and the worst ones used her dependence to control her and get her to do whatever they wanted. But even those guys left her, and then she was always fucked because she couldn't handle even the most basic shit."

I nod, reaching out to place my hands on his waist.

"She could never take care of herself, so she couldn't take care of us either. I knew, even as a little kid, that having to rely on other people wasn't smart. You have to be able to take care of things on your own. But I took it too far. I've never trusted anyone for anything. I could never let anyone in because I needed to make sure I could handle everything alone. But I've figured out that sometimes it's okay to get help. I know I can handle things alone, but I don't have to. I can accept help."

I smile at him. "Yeah. And not everyone who wants to help you will leave you."

"I know that too now, thanks to you and your family. Being around you guys, watching how you are together, taught me that not everyone will leave when things get tough. I never believed that before."

"And now what do you believe?" I ask him, pulling him closer to me. When I look into his eyes, I see the trust in them.

"Now I believe the good ones will stick around. And I don't know how it happened, but I believe I somehow got lucky enough to find one of those good ones."

CHAPTER 34

TYLER

Sam's eyes grow round for a moment as he takes in my words, and then his face breaks into that amazing smile of his, the one that makes you feel like you're standing in the sunshine, letting it warm your face. He pulls me even closer so I'm pressed up against him. "Where'd you manage to find this so-called good one?" he says teasingly.

"Oddly enough, he's been right in front of me for a while now. I was just too busy with other things to see him. But I see him now, and I really want to keep seeing him. I know there are no guarantees, and he might have to move away, and things might get hard. But I still really want to keep seeing him."

"He wants that too." Sam's eyes are shiny as he reaches up to meet my mouth in a gentle kiss.

When we break apart, he pulls back so he can search my face. "I promise, you can always depend on me, Tyler. But you'll never need me the way your mother needed those men. You're already proven that over and over again. But I'll always be there if you want my help."

We share another kiss, this one longer and sexier. And when we pull apart, we're both breathless, grinning at each other like a couple of idiots.

"Wait, wait, I have news for you before we get too carried away with other things." The look on Sam's face reminds me of a little kid who's trying to hold in a big secret, like they might explode with excitement.

"Oh? Do tell."

"So, I had dinner with my cousins last night. It turns out that part of the reason Mason has been acting a little weird was because he's been planning and plotting something big. When we're done with the Ocean Shores job, Mason and Dylan want me to open a Hot Dam Homes office in Oregon. I'm buying in as a full partner. Mason, Dylan, and I will be completely equal co-owners." His eyes are sparkling with excitement.

"Oh my god, really? So that means you're staying? You're not going to move to California?"

He shakes his head. "Nope. I talked to my buddy last night and told him I'm staying here—well, in the Pacific Northwest, anyway."

"Oh my god, that makes me so happy!" Now I'm the one who feels like I might burst with excitement.

Sam laughs, lifting me up by the waist and spinning me around. When he sets me down, he presses a kiss onto my mouth, and I feel giddy. I can't believe this is my life. Sam is the most amazing thing to ever happen to me, and we're going to get a real chance to make this thing work between us. I know we're going to make mistakes, but I also know in my heart that Sam is nothing like my mother. He's already shown me I can trust him to be there when I need him, and I'm going to do the same for him. I'm excited as hell to find out what we can build together, and I can't wait to get started.

Epilogue

SAM – About One Year Later

The late-spring sun is shining down on us as Tyler and I stand on the beach, looking up at the main lodge building. Mason and Dylan will be arriving soon, and later on, the rest of the Hot Dam Homes family will be showing up.

It's been just over a year since we began the hotel project. As the project went on, it grew in scope, as the owner was so happy with everything we were doing. Finishing it took longer than we'd first thought, but it's been incredibly satisfying to watch the old property come back to life. And of course, having this year with Tyler has been amazing. I've never felt more confident, both in myself and in my relation-ship. Tyler shows me every day how much he loves me and how perfect we are for each other. Without a doubt, it's been the best year of my life.

The resort will welcome its first official guests in time for the summer season, but this week-end is a special soft opening. The owner is so thrilled with how everything turned out he of-fered to host the entire HDH family, including spouses and children, for a weekend so the staff can "practice" on us before the paying guests show up.

"It looks amazing, don't you think?" I ask, squeezing his hand.

He squeezes back, giving me a huge smile. "It's incredible. It almost makes me want to stay in this industry."

That comment earns him an eyebrow raise, and he laughs. "Almost. I said almost..." He leans into my shoulder.

Earlier this year, Tyler and Aaron managed to pay off the remaining balance on their moth-er's debt, a welcome end to that chapter in their lives. Aaron made the permanent move to Nashville a couple of months ago, and he's al-ready worked with several well-known country music stars. He's thrilled with the direction his career is going.

Because the coast project took longer than planned, we held off on opening the Oregon office until it was done. Which means after this weekend, Tyler and I are headed down to our new home in Portland instead of back to Seattle. We've found a gorgeous old Craftsman house to rent, and the owner is giving us an incredible deal in exchange for us doing a few upgrades and repairs around the place.

Tyler is finally going to use his GI bill and go back to school to become an art teacher. He'll be starting work on his bachelor's degree, and after that, he'll be able to get into an education program. It took some work, and more than a little bribery, but I convinced him to go to school full-time and let me handle our living expenses. I know he has reservations about quitting his job, still never wanting to become dependent on me, but every day, his trust in me grows. He knows he's it for me. I'm never going anywhere.

"We did good, you know that?" I say as we head toward the beach stairs to climb back up.

"Yeah, we did." He smiles and leans over to kiss my cheek.

Mason and Jackson's white SUV is pulling up as we get to the top of the stairs. "Oh shit, brace yourself," I say, laughing.

Their twins, Alexander and Gwendolyne, are almost six months old. I have to say, Mason and Jax have both handled the chaos better than I imagined they would. Watching them gives me a lot of hope for what our own future family might be. Tyler and I both want that, but we're okay to wait a few years until our lives are a little more settled.

Mason hops out of the SUV and opens the rear gate, letting loose Harry and Sally. The dogs immediately head straight for Tyler and me, jumping on us and begging for affection, which we're happy to provide.

"Hey, guys," Mason calls as he starts unloading the massive amount of *stuff* they have to travel with nowadays. It turns out babies, especially two of them, need a ridiculous amount of *stuff*. Everything from diapers and bottles to special swings, playpens for them to sleep in, portable high chairs, toys. The list goes on and on. But I've never seen either of them so happy, and it fills my sappy heart with joy.

TYLER

Shortly after we get Mason, Jax, and the twins settled, Dylan and Reed show up, and the rest of the crowd begins arriving in a steady stream after that.

A couple of hours later, everyone is gathered in the great room. The hotel staff is incredible, the champagne is flowing, and they make sure no one is ever without a drink and one of the delicious appetizers to nibble on.

This room is my favorite place on the whole property. It's two stories high, with floor-to-ceiling windows facing the ocean. Right now, a crackling fire is burning in the big river-rock fireplace. The sun is starting to set, and the water glows as the sky begins to change to brilliant pink and orange. Rolling waves crash against the shore, creeping up the beach as far as they can before retreating.

An arm snakes around my waist, and Sam sidles up beside me, pulling me into him before placing a kiss on my temple.

"All good here?" he asks.

I turn to face him fully and loop my arms around his neck. "I'm better than good." I lean in and place a soft kiss on his mouth, and we exchange soft smiles, resting our foreheads together.

"I love you," Sam says, and like always, my heart flutters in my chest when he says the words. We say it to each other all the time, and my pulse speeds up every time.

I can't believe this is my life now. I never could have dreamed I'd end up here. I can honestly say everything I've been through in my entire life was worth it because it led me to where I am now.

Aaron and I took a few days away last summer to spread our mom's ashes over the ocean, and we spent a long time talking about what we lived through. I feel closer and more connected to him now than I ever have, and I think we've both reconciled our relationships with her. Our mother was a difficult person, full of flaws. She wasn't strong enough to deal with her life, and we paid the price. But it made us both strong, and we know how much we can handle without breaking.

Sam is the most incredible thing that's ever happened to me, and he's helped me to see that even though I'm able to handle everything on my own, I don't have to, and letting someone support me and love me isn't a sign of weakness. Both Aaron and I have been welcomed into the Campbell family with open arms. At first, it was awkward, neither one of us knowing how to be part of a family. But they're amazingly patient and kind, and I know Aaron loves them as much as I do.

Sam used to believe he was too ordinary. I still don't agree. Maybe our lives won't be written about in history books hundreds of years from now, but in this ordinary life, Sam and I are building an extraordinary love, and I wouldn't trade it for anything.

· · · · ●·●· · ·

Thank you for reading _**Built To Last**_. I hope you loved Sam & Tyler's story.

Have you read all the Hot Dam Homes books?
**From The Ground Up** is Mason & Jackson's steamy, celebrity & blue collar guy story.
https://mybook.to/ftgu
In _**When The Walls Come Down**_ Dylan & Reed in get their unlikely but worth-the-wait happily ever after.
https://mybook.to/wwcd
All books are available in Kindle Unlimited.

You'll love my new ***Seattle Sasquatch Hockey*** series. Book One: ***Rylan***Available at

https://mybook.to/rylan

· · · ● · ● ● · · ·

Keep up with all Harper Robson's news & info on sales and more goodies by signing up for the VIP newsletter at https://www.subscribepage.com/harpernewsletter

A Note From Harper

Thank you so very much for reading *Built To Last*. If you want more from the *Hot Dam Homes* world, check out the list of other books and stories on the next page!

I want to thank my amazing tribe of M/M authors (do I sound like I'm making an Oscar speech? I'll try to keep it short so the orchestra doesn't play me off.) LD Blakely, Michaela Cole, Matthew Dante, Jeris Jean, SM Landon, Duckie Mack, Garry Michael, Michael Robert, and Kota Quinn. You are all amazing people and incredible writers. I'm lucky and happy to be able to call you my friends.

My real life friends, my Coven of autism-moms, are the most amazing, supportive group of people in the world. I love you all so much, and it doesn't matter how many miles are between us, you're my rocks. Thank you. To my sister from another mother, CarrieB, I love you so, so much. Whether it's a weekend jaunt to Chicago or a texting marathon to discuss the excruciating minutiae of our lives, you're always there for me, and I love you. I can't wait for our next trip.

Thanks to Julia and Sandra, from One Love Editing, without whom I can't imagine trying to do this. Thanks also to Cate for the beautiful cover, you always do such amazing work. Save those airline miles, ladies, that poolside writing retreat in San Diego awaits you!

A very special thanks to Roger Robb, who made himself available to answer my questions about the d/Deaf community and teach me how people with hearing differences do things hearing people take for granted. Thank you so much, Roger!

Finally, thank you so much to you, readers. I love being able to write stories and I love hearing you've enjoyed reading them. I never truly believed I'd ever be able to call myself a writer. But thanks to you all, I do, and it makes me so happy!

I hope you enjoyed Sam & Tyler's story. I'd love to hear your thoughts. You can always email me at harper@harperrobson.com or find me on social media. And if you enjoyed the book, I'd be super grateful if you left a review on Amazon or elsewhere. Reviews make a huge difference to Indie authors, so thank you for taking the time!

Until next time,

Love & light,

xo Harper

June 2023, Chilliwack, BC

ALSO BY HARPER ROBSON

· · · • · • · · ·

The Getaways Series

Making Waves: Hunter & Penn https://myboo
k.to/makingwaves

Making Waves Audiobook: Narrated by Kevin
Earlywine & Cole Michael Kurcz
available at shop.harperrobson.com

Love After Love: Martin & Jesse (a Getaways
Novella) https://mybook.to/loveafterlove

· · • • · • • · · ·

The Seattle Sasquatch Series

Rylan: Book One https://mybook.to/rylan
Louis: Book Two (2025) https://mybook.to/lou
Austin: Book Three (2025)
Carson: Book Four (2026)

Part of the *Seattle Sasquatch* World

The Night Before: Aleks & Ben https://myboo
k.to/thenightbefore
A *Seattle Sasquatch Hockey* Christmas Prequel
Novel

**All books are available on Amazon and
in Kindle Unlimited (unless otherwise
noted)**

ALL ABOUT HARPER ROBSON

Harper Robson grew up dreaming about being a writer someday. That someday didn't arrive until she was in her mid-forties–but better late than never! While traveling that long and winding road, she worked in marketing, software development, the oil & gas industry and spent more than a decade as a stay-home mom. She grew up in Vancouver, BC, but feels most at home in the leafy green suburbs of Seattle, Washington. In 2023, Harper and her clan pulled up stakes and headed south to live in San Diego, California. She was certain she'd miss the rainy, gray days of the Pacific Northwest, but it turns out regular doses of sunshine and palm trees are pretty easy to get used to, and San Diego feels more like home every day.

She's a mom to two teenaged boys and an adorable but naughty yellow Labrador Retriever. Her husband works in the tech industry and he makes her laugh every single day.

A true PNW girl, Harper loves the rain but is always planning her next beach vacation. Her favorite things include road trips, classic rock, the Seattle Kraken, her dogs, and drinking champagne for no reason at all.

She would love to hear from you anytime! Email her at harper@harperrobson.com

Visit harperrobson.com and sign up for the Newsletter

Let's Connect!

The best way to keep up with all things Harper is to sign up for the VIP Newsletter: https://www.subscribepage.com/harpernewsletter

• • • • • • • • • •

Bluesky: @harperrobsonauthor.bsky.social
Facebook: Harper Robson
Instagram: @harperrobsonauthor
BookBub: @harperrobsonauthor
Facebook Group: Harper's Heartbreakers: https://www.facebook.com/groups/harpersheartbreakers

• • • • • • • • • •

Goodreads:
https://www.goodreads.com/author/show/222
84469.Harper_Robson

· · • • · • • • · ·

Amazon Author Page
https://www.amazon.com/author/harperrobso
n

· · • • · • • • · ·

Website: www.harperrobson.com

GET YOUR FREE BOOK!

Head over to
www.subscribepage.com/harperbackmatter
to sign up for my VIP newsletter. You'll receive a free copy of *A Clean Slate,* Eric and Drew's steamy, age-gap love story.

Eric

I've been dealing with a chronic illness since I was nine years old, and, believe me, it's a drag. Being a Type 1 diabetic affects every relationship in my life, from my parents all the way through the guys I date. After getting unceremoniously dumped because of it, I've decided that romantic relationships aren't in the cards for me. The last thing I want is to be a burden on anyone. But when my best friend drags me to a weekend memorial for his grandmother and I meet his uncle, I start to wonder if he means it when he tells me I could never be a burden.

Drew

Being a single, gay man in New York city and making a decent living as a writer isn't a bad gig. But after the end of a long-term relationship, I'm at a crossroads. I can stay here and continue on with life as I know it, or I can take this opportunity to make a big change and start over in a new place. I've spent my entire adult life resisting change, but when I travel across the country for my mother's memorial weekend, I meet someone who makes me think that jumping in with both feet might not be the worst decision. The problem is, he's my nephew's best friend, and he's half my age.

A Clean Slate is a steamy, age-gap romance featuring a New York City-based writer and a West Coast Ph.D student who probably shouldn't fit together, but somehow do.